She retrieved her ~~~ ill
mound of material, h
the gentleman's necl
she threaded her fing
locks, easing the tousl

"Uh! No!" the ma attempted to rise but fell back down wit groan, taking several deep, ragged breaths. The thick eyelashes framing his eyelids suddenly fluttered and opened wide.

Sophia gazed into a pair of well-remembered piercing green eyes. "Sir Edward!"

"I…It's you!" he muttered. "Wh…what…?"

"Shhh. It is best not to attempt to speak." She tried to shift to a more comfortable position, but he winced at the sudden movement. She held herself as still as possible. "I will tell you what little I know."

"My lady! Whatever are you about?" Josephine sat up in a rigid posture, staring at her.

"Do not be concerned." Sophia twisted around to frown at her maid. "We are acquainted. I am explaining as best I can what happened."

"Your…your despotic companion?" he queried, with a weak chuckle.

"Thankfully, no," she countered. "Merely my fretful lady's maid."

"Ah." He sighed. "A singular individual in a position to be only slightly less irritating."

"Indeed." She moved one hand away from his head to grip his shoulder. "Now please, be quiet and listen to me. You must conserve your strength."

"I am yours to command," he uttered before groaning, closing his eyes as the coach suddenly lurched.

Other Books by Cynthia Moore

Banished to Berkshire

by

Cynthia Moore

Road to Romance, Book 2

Banished to Berkshire

Cover Art by *Tina Lynn Stout*

The Wild Rose Press, Inc.
PO Box 708
Adams Basin, NY 14410-0708
Visit us at www.thewildrosepress.com

Publishing History
First Edition, 2022
Trade Paperback ISBN 978-1-5092-4134-7
Digital ISBN 978-1-5092-4135-4

Road to Romance, Book 2
Published in the United States of America

Dedication

To my dear father,
who reserved a bookshelf in his office
for a place to display my books
and the pictures of me signing them at conferences.
I love you and miss you so much!

Prologue

London, Mid-June 1819

"We must go, Sophia." Her mother murmured the words through stiff lips rooted into a semblance of a smile.

They made their way through the crowded ballroom, passing many people. Some were openly staring. Other attendees glanced at them before turning away. Several young women giggled behind their gloved hands. Lady Sophia Hampton kept her chin raised and her gaze trained on the open double doors in front of her, allowing nothing but a blank expression to appear on her face. Sophia and her mother reached the entry after what felt like an eternity but was only a matter of minutes. A footman stood near the front door with both of their pelisses draped over his arm. After helping don their garments, the butler informed them their carriage had been requested and would be arriving momentarily.

They walked down the marble steps to the front drive. Her mother made a jerking motion with her hand, reaching up to touch her neck.

"Oh! I have forgotten my scarf. Wait here. I will return in a moment."

Sophia nodded. She stared straight ahead at the dense shrubbery bordering the sidewalk across the street from the mansion. The unwelcome sound of rumbling, male voices suddenly intruded upon her reverie. She winced, glancing around for a place to hide. Moments later, a group of several gentlemen appeared. Thankfully, they seemed caught up in their own concerns and none of them looked her way. She was just congratulating herself on her close escape when one of the men, at the back of the cluster, turned and glanced in her direction.

"Lady Sophia?" He broke away from the group, striding forward, before abruptly turning around and calling to the others, "Carry on! I will catch up with you."

He strolled toward her, stopping a few feet away, bowing. "It is a pleasure to see you again."

"Sir Edward." She curtsied to him, cringing inwardly as she noted her voice resembled the sound of a croaking frog. She cleared her throat. "I would have thought you would be content never to see me again after my *faux paus* last summer. Lady Collins was certainly annoyed. I did enjoy our game of billiards."

"An event I will always remember with delight," he agreed. "Looking back, my mother had cause to be thankful for the uneven numbers. An extra gentleman at country house parties can quickly turn into a benefit to be celebrated."

She smiled at him, relishing the momentary sensation of being appreciated. "I trust you are correct. It would be an immense relief to know she had pardoned me."

"I have overlooked the matter and bear no malice," he attested with a grin, his intense green eyes glowing. "Frankly, I admit I was not surprised. Word of your outrageous behavior in finishing school preceded your visit. My sister related several tales of your shocking conduct there."

Her cheeks were hot, and she was grateful for the muted light. "Of course. Camille would relish describing all aspects of my improper behavior."

He tilted his head to one side, studying her. "I must track down my friends. I am happy I had a chance to speak to you. Good-bye."

"Good-bye."

Her mother joined her moments later. As if on que, their carriage swept around the bend, rolling to a stop in front of them. A groomsman strode forward, opening the door and lowering the steps. Sophia followed her mother inside, reclining back against the seat opposite her with a sigh.

"I doubt your father will have returned from his club. It is still early," Lady Breech remarked with a frown.

"I plan to read in my bedchamber before I retire for the night," Sophia informed her.

"Shouldn't you stay up until he comes home and explain what occurred at the ball?"

Sophia put a hand in front of her face in an unsuccessful attempt to stifle a yawn. "I doubt such a mundane incident would be of any interest to him."

Her mother raised her brows. "I am certain word of what happened will spread like wildfire throughout the city in the next few hours."

"More evidence of how little London society values other people's privacy."

"Rather, affirmation London society cannot resist disseminating tantalizing bits of gossip, no matter how trivial," her mother countered in a somber tone."

****

"I am certain you know why we requested your presence here this morning, Daughter." The Marquess of Breech frowned down at the carpeted floor, clasping his hands behind his back, as he paced back and forth in front of the fireplace in the sitting room.

Sophia sat up straight in her chair. It was easier to see her reflection in the large mirror hanging above her mother's worktable. She patted one smooth, opalescent cheek while she studied her appearance before turning around. "Honestly, I cannot imagine why you wished to talk to me, Father."

Lord Breech halted his movement mid-stride, looking at her with raised brows. "You mean to feign ignorance?"

She turned back to the mirror, moving her head to one side in order to inspect the cluster of silky black curls gathered at the crown of her head. She coaxed a wayward strand into place with one finger. "I am not pretending bewilderment. Pray, enlighten me. What is it you wish to speak to me about?"

He made a choking sound in his throat, before turning to his wife. "I understood *our* daughter kissed Lord Dunson in front of his betrothed last evening. Am I wrong?"

"Of course not, dear." Lady Breech stood up from her chair, smoothing the wrinkles from her riding habit before addressing her offspring. "Your father is referring to the misunderstanding last night at the Covington ball."

"Oh." Sophia hastily gave up the preoccupation with her image and faced her father. "I am not to blame."

Her father scowled. "I am certain you will forgive my presumption if say I find your statement hard to believe."

She frowned at him. "I assure you I speak the truth, Father. Lady Covington expected the prince to make an appearance last night. You know how sensitive the Regent is to drafts. She instructed her servants to light dozens of candles and to build up the fires in all the downstairs chambers. The ball was a crush, the rooms full of people and stifling hot. I could hardly breathe and stepped out onto the balcony for some fresh air. Lord Dunson suddenly appeared, wrapped his arms around my shoulders, and kissed me."

"You allowed him to embrace you?" He snarled the words and his eyebrows lowered in one thick, quivering line over his eyes. "Why did you not turn away and return to the ballroom?"

"He caught me by surprise." The even timbre of her voice rose as her feelings of frustration increased. She took a deep breath to calm herself before continuing, "I could not free myself. Enveloped by his muscular arms, there was no possibility of escape. He had expected his betrothed to meet him outside."

His face flushed a deep red, and he balled his hands into tight fists at his sides as he barked out his reply. "Surely he understood he cornered the wrong woman?"

An unladylike grunt emerged from her mouth. "Not until Lady Louisa stepped onto the terrace behind me and began to wail."

"Unfortunately, Lady Covington stood nearby, and she made haste to discover the cause of her guest's distress," her mother clarified, as she walked across the room to stand next to her husband, putting a hand on his arm. "She came upon the three of them, quickly making up her own mind as to what occurred."

"What of Lord Rambolt?" he questioned, compellingly.

"Lord...Rambolt?" Sophia repeated the name, with apprehension, as she remembered her introduction to the Earl a fortnight ago. More than twice her age, his breath smelled of rotten cabbage. She constricted her stomach muscles, taking cursory breaths to avoid nausea while he spoke to her. His clothing carried a damp, musty odor as if the garments had never dried properly. The gentleman also sported a large nose with a sizable wart perched on the tip. During their brief conversation, she had to remind herself not to stare at it. Their discourse was largely one-sided. Lord Rambolt informed her of the passing of his wife almost two years ago. She left behind a full nursery, two boys and three girls: the eldest, a boy, twelve years old, the youngest a girl of four.

She shuddered, remembering his parting comment to her, "*I am aware you are an only child, Lady Sophia, but your mother's sister has a healthy brood of children. It stands to reason you could add a few more to my own flock.*"

"No, no, Father!" she pleaded, making no attempt to hide her feelings of revulsion.

He studied her without speaking for several moments. Then he shook her mother's hand off his arm and cleared his throat. "Do I need to remind you that you will be twenty-one in a few months' time, considered firmly on the shelf in society's eyes? I paid stacks upon stacks of bills for slippers, parasols, hats, gloves, reticules, and gowns and turned a blind eye to the giddy, frivolous manner in which you approached the Season. I never commented on your ploys of feigned ignorance of the fundamental requirement to secure a titled husband before you were believed to be past your prime and never questioned your ongoing friendship with Sir Raeford. Since he has yet to approach me, I assume he will never be a serious contender for your hand. You squandered the chance to marry Lord Millington last year and now this fiasco occurs with Lord Dunson. You refuse to consider any eligible gentleman we bring to your notice. My patience with your behavior is at an end. Your time in London is over. I leave your mother to explain our immediate plans for you."

Chapter One

Bucklebury, Berkshire, late June 1819

Sir Edward Collins dug his heels into Seymour's flanks. His horse responded by cantering up the elongated byway leading to the house. Within minutes, he cleared the rise, the main entrance spread out before him. When a husky boy dressed in groom's attire came running into the driveway from a pathway behind the house sheltered by several large trees, he pulled back on the reins. The animal slowed to a trot and then a walk before ambling to a stop.

"Thank you," he acknowledged the lad as he handed him the reins. Edward swung his leg over the saddle, dropping to the ground, pausing to arch his back and stretch his stiff limbs. "Rub him down well and give him some fresh hay. He worked especially hard over the last few miles."

"Yes, sir." The boy doffed his cap to him before leading his horse away toward the stables.

He took a minute to study the trees surrounding the drive. Their trunks were framed by beds of blooming flowers, waving gently in the early morning summer breeze. The three-storied red brick house with white cornices and dormer windows cast a warm glow across the entire front landscape. He adjusted his hat securely on his tousled black hair, gathered his gloves together in one hand, and strode up the graveled walkway to the front door. It opened before he could raise his hand to knock.

"Tolbert, how are you?" he greeted the portly butler standing in the entry. "Is your master at home?"

"Sir Edward!" The elderly retainer cleared his throat. "Is Lord Millington expecting you?"

He grinned. "No. I made a spur of the moment decision."

Tolbert sighed before replying. "Many pardons, but Lord and Lady Millington are together in the morning room. I need to first ascertain if they are prepared to receive guests."

"What?" He stared at the butler with raised brows before suddenly realizing his mistake. "Oh, yes. They are but lately married. I quite understand."

"Indeed." The normally imperturbable man frowned severely before pressing his lips together. "Please wait here. I will return in a moment."

"Very well." Edward whistled a bawdy tune to reassure himself as the butler hurried away. It hadn't been a capital notion to drop in on Lucas, but there was no help for it now. He paced back and forth across the marble tile floor in the entry, stopping to peruse a painting hanging over the hall table featuring a frigate sailing on a choppy sea.

"Edward!" His longtime friend, Lucas Carter, Viscount Millington burst into the entry and slapped him on the back. "I could not believe what I heard when Tolbert informed me you were here."

"Well met, Lucas!" Edward replied, as he openly studied his staunch companion from Eton college days. He looked relaxed and happy. "I am sorry for intruding upon you like this."

"Intruding? You surely are aware you are always welcome here."

He grinned at his friend. "I must admit I forgot you were married and stopped out of habit."

Lucas chuckled. "I am not surprised. It did take an inordinate amount of time for me to settle down."

"You look like the change in your lifestyle agrees with you," he remarked.

"Yes, it certainly does," Lucas countered with a smile. "Leave your things with Tolbert. Come, say hello to Emma. We were just sitting down to breakfast. You are welcome to join us."

He mulled over Lucas' comments as he followed him down the hallway. It was difficult to imagine, just over a year ago, his friend lamented the fact his parents were bedeviling him over his continued bachelor state and giving him an ultimatum to marry.

Lucas reached a door at the end of the hall, opening it to reveal a cozy interior adorned with a writing desk in the far corner of the room by the window, two upholstered armchairs flanking a roaring fire in the center. Adjacent to this, four high-backed chairs were drawn up to a square table holding several covered dishes and a large teapot. An elderly foxhound reclined on the floor nearby. "My dear, here is our visitor."

"Edward!" Lady Millington stood up from one of the armchairs, dropping the embroidery frame she held onto the floor. She hurried across the carpet to confront him. "It is so very good to see you."

He grasped her outstretched hands, bowing his head before her warm gaze. "I hope you still feel that way after you hear my explanation for being here. I confessed to Lucas, I failed to remember his recent nuptials and came to visit without further consideration."

"Gracious! Do not fret so." She gently squeezed his fingers. "Lucas and I were married over three months ago. We spent plenty of time on our own."

He raised up to look directly into her brown eyes and grinned at her. "Are you longing for someone else to entertain you on the long, summer evenings?"

She laughed, dropping his hands before turning to Lucas. "Now you are coming on too strong! I cannot imagine ever getting tired of my husband's companionship."

"I will never give you reason to, my dear," Lucas vowed, bending over to place a kiss on the tip her nose.

"Well, that point is settled." She smiled at her husband before reaching out to clutch his sleeve. "Should I speak to Cook about adding one more place for breakfast?"

Lucas turned to him. "You are staying over tonight?"

"No, sorry. I will share your meal." Edward studied them both before continuing in a somber tone, "It is not possible to prolong my visit. I need to return to my estate."

Lucas draped his wife's hand over his arm. "I will add to Emma's previous statements and assure you are welcome to stay as long as you wish."

"Please consider it, Edward. I will return shortly. Come, Barker." She turned away, walking toward the door. The dog stood up, slowly stretching himself before strolling over to follow his mistress.

As the door closed behind them, Lucas bent over to

pick up his wife's embroidery frame, placing it on the desktop. "Sit down. I trust your carriage is safely stowed in my stables?"

They settled themselves in the armchairs before Edward clarified, "Actually, I sent my coach with Hawkes and most of my baggage on to Horsham House. I rode Seymour here."

Lucas raised his brows. "I can imagine Hawkes' reaction to your plans. Your valet is known to fret whenever he is forced to leave you to your own devices. Did you come from London? That is quite a long distance, even for such a prime horse as Seymour."

"You are correct. I spent some time in the city." He grimaced. "Tired of being cooped up inside stuffy drawing rooms and crowded ballrooms, having visited them both with alarming regularity over the past several weeks, I yearned for fresh air and decided to ride my horse home. Last night was spent in Reading."

Lucas grinned. "Very obliging to yourself and your horse. You speak of *stuffy drawing rooms and crowded ballrooms*. Do I sense Lady Collins' machinations at play?"

"You understand the situation." He sighed. "I promised my mother to attend a few balls this season and spent almost two months in London."

Lucas frowned at him. "You left before the season officially ended. No young lady sparked your interest?"

He grunted before answering. "Marriage is a very serious undertaking. The woman I choose will be a part of my life until death. I refuse to be rushed into asking for an arbitrary lady's hand. It is important to have her absolute trust and unconditional loyalty, something impossible to discover after a few hours at a ball. Every time I vow to concentrate on finding a suitable woman, a crisis occurs on my estate that requires my immediate attention, or my banker, lawyer, or steward informs me of an essential document that needs my signature without delay."

"Indeed. You certainly set a high bar for your possible contenders. I assure you, your lament is not falling on deaf ears. You must not be distracted by other concerns when making such a crucial decision." His friend clasped his hands together in his lap, facing forward, without speaking for a moment. "Perhaps you should go further afield in your quest for a wife? There are other places in Great Britain to find eligible women. Although initially we met by chance in London, my official introduction to Emma took place in Brighton, after all."

Edward stroked his chin with his thumb while he stared into the fire. "You might be on to something there. While in the metropolis, I wasted much time, initially put off by the sense of desperation surrounding match-making mothers as well as their daughters. It would be interesting to learn how many women are in London giving the marriage mart one last try before resigning themselves to spinsterhood."

Lucas grimaced. "We are both well aware of the enormous pressure placed on our shoulders to follow the rigid line of society's rules. We also observe many a family in straightened circumstances retreat almost penniless to their country homes, after failing to secure an advantageous marriage for their daughters during the season."

The door behind them opened wide to reveal the

lady of the house, followed by the butler, carrying a large silver tray containing a plate, silverware, and another covered dish.

With a swish of her skirts, she swiftly crossed the floor pointing to the table. "Thank you, Tolbert. Please arrange a place for our guest."

The butler did as she requested and then bowed himself out of the room.

"I instructed Cook to make a few more boiled eggs as well as a rasher of bacon." She sat down at the table reaching for the teapot. "There is plenty of bread and marmalade."

"It looks delightful, Lady Millington." He settled himself next to his hostess while Lucas sat across from his wife.

She stopped pouring the tea to look at him with an arrested expression on her face. "Why are you being so formal, Edward? Please call me Emma."

"Very well, Emma." He chuckled. "I forgot myself."

"Rather," Lucas drawled, with a grin. "Did you also forget you were my groomsman at our wedding? We are all family here."

She handed Edward his cup. "Tell me, are you returning to your estate from London? Did you make the trip there for business or pleasure?"

"Yes, to your first query." He lifted the lids off a couple of dishes, helping himself to some eggs and bacon. "In answer to the second question, it was a visit of personal concern. I attempted to search for a possible candidate to fulfill the position of my wife."

She passed a cup to Lucas. "How melancholy you make the process sound! I trust you made an appearance at a few balls while you were there?"

"As a matter of fact, I attended several assemblies, balls, and dinner parties. It was certainly a hectic visit." He scowled. "With no opportunity for serious discourse, I met no one I could ever consider marrying."

She took a sip of her tea, studying him over the rim. "What of Lady Sophia Hampton? I remember the time the four of us played billiards at your house party last summer. I sensed the two of you were intrigued by each other. Did you happen to see her while you were in London?"

Lucas chewed on a piece of bacon and cleared his throat before speaking. "Why in the world do you mention her, my dear? You never absolved me for asking you to ride in a carriage with her for several hours on the trip to Edward's house!"

"Nonsense, I forgave you for arranging that bit of torment long ago."

"I am very relieved to hear you say so." Lucas reached for his wife's hand, kissing her palm.

Edward swallowed a piece of egg and stared blankly at the far wall before replying. "To answer your question, I saw Lady Sophia a few days ago."

The knife Emma was using to butter her toast fell from her fingers, clattering onto her plate. "Were you attending a ball? Did you dance with her?"

"No. The circumstances were awkward." He picked up a piece of bacon before continuing, "She was standing by herself in front of the Covington mansion."

"She was alone?" Emma asked with brows raised. "Did you inquire how she happened to be in such a troublesome state?"

"I considered questioning the cause," he concurred, with a frown. "However, there was only a moment to speak with her. I observed her when strolling with several acquaintances to Boodle's. I told the others to go ahead and promised to catch up with them."

"I can hazard a guess at the reason," Lucas announced, with a smug expression on his face. "Recall Lady Sophia's grand entrance at your house party, Edward, putting us all in the uncomfortable, undesirable position of admiring her. What about the colossal nerve and imprudence she displayed when she invited her dear friend Sir Raeford to attend the party without asking Lady Collins' permission, my dear?"

Emma shuddered as she reached for her cup and took a sip of tea. "I will never forget how angry I was at her absolute, uncaring presumption."

"She certainly came off as vain and full of self-importance," Edward agreed, choosing not to divulge her recent confessions of regret to him to the others. He was not very well acquainted with Lady Sophia. Perhaps her apology was not genuine, and it had simply been a way to sooth her own vanity.

"Then neither of you will be surprised if I tell you I believe Lady Sophia did something scandalous at the Covington ball," Lucas declared. "It was so contemptible she was asked to leave. For that reason, she made her appearance alone at the front of the house, waiting for a conveyance to take her home."

"Hmmm. It is certainly a possibility," Emma conceded. "I would question your reasoning if we were discussing almost any other woman, but I have first-hand knowledge Lady Sophia is capable of abominable behavior."

Edward sat back in his chair as he pondered Lucas' suspicions. "I wonder if there is any correlation to the fact that I never saw Lady Sophia at balls or social events while I was in London? Could something scurrilous have occurred to her weeks ago?"

"Doubtful," Emma reasoned. "She would have retired to the country in that case. The fact she attended the Covington ball is a validation that she was still in Society's good graces. Many events often take place on the same evening. Perhaps you both attended different gatherings and never chanced upon one another."

"I am very surprised I never encountered her," he replied, thoughtfully. "Women like her make a point to grace numerous diversions during the season with their presence."

"*Women like her*?" Lucas grinned at him. "You mean to say a woman completely caught up in herself and her appearance?"

Emma giggled. "I certainly agree she can be tedious at times, but we should reserve judgement until we find out what happened at the Covington ball. I believe there is more to her than what she shows to society and the outside world."

"Of course there is!" Lucas laughed. "However, I must point out it is extremely doubtful Lady Sophia would ever disrobe in public."

"Lucas!" She playfully rapped her husband's arm before turning to gaze intently at Edward. "I believe the attraction I sensed between the two of you could easily grow into something of a more serious nature."

"Now that is a ridiculous notion!" he countered, aware of a deep-seated sense of panic at the bottom of his stomach. "Last summer I found myself bored with time on my hands and unattached females present. There was ample opportunity to liven up the dreary atmosphere with a bit of lighthearted flirtation. That is what you observed. She holds absolutely no appeal for me."

Chapter Two

Lady Sophia Hampton rested her head back against the carriage seat, listening to the rumble of the wheels rolling across the rough, country road. She stared up at the ceiling, contemplating the future. Her scheme to insure she never captured the interest of any eligible gentleman had worked rather too well. Before evening, she would arrive at South Hill Park in Bracknell, Berkshire, for an extended sojourn, at the residence of her mother's sister, Mrs. Joan Canning and her four children. Her husband happened to be the illustrious government official, Mr. George Canning. She stayed with her aunt once before, the summer she turned twelve. She recalled the interior of the house itself was quite cozy and comfortable. However, the entire estate covered thirty acres. The surrounding area could easily be called remote, even isolated. She understood her uncle George rarely came home to visit his family, his current duties as President of the Board of Control required his perpetuating presence in London. Her aunt certainly would not hold gatherings or convivial events in order to further her husband's career in his absence. This meant Sophia needn't be preoccupied with the question of how best to maneuver social situations to give men a disgust of her. There would be few, if any, cordial visits.

The carriage swayed, then bounced and shook. She

gripped the leather strap attached to side of the door. What started as a light drizzle an hour ago, had turned into blinding sheets of heavy rain pounding relentlessly against the windows. She sat up, turning toward the window to peer outside. She observed the daylight rapidly fading. She made out a few sodden trees and shrubs bordering the road. "I hope the glass vials I brought with me do not break. I am not certain when I will return to town. I gave my entire supply of face tonic to Mr. Hoover yesterday. I will have to create more soon and send it to town on the mail coach."

"I made certain the bottles were well wrapped, my lady. They should be fine," her lady's maid, Josephine called out over the storm's wrath from the opposite corner of the carriage.

She had good reason to trust her. Josephine had been with her since shortly after Sophia turned fifteen when the death of Josephine's father meant she had to find employment to help support her mother and grandmother. She approached Sophia and her mother one day when they were leaving a modiste's shop in London and beseeched them for any type of commission or chore. Sophia's heart had gone out to the desperate young woman and her plight. She entreated her mother to allow her to hire her as her lady's maid.

Their relationship had evolved into one of delicate balance. While maintaining the respectful distance required between employer and employee, there was an undercurrent of gratitude and appreciation for each other as well.

"How much farther do we have to go, my lady?" shouted Josephine.

Sophia thrust her free hand into a pocket on her gown, pulling out an intricate chain. Her time piece was attached to it. She squinted to read the tiny dials in the dim light. "It is a little after three o'clock. We left Slough at noon. John informed me it was twenty miles to Bracknell from there. With this storm, we will be lucky to arrive by four o'clock."

"It is getting cold, my lady." Her maid pulled the blanket draped across her lap up under her chin.

"Muse on the roast beef, potatoes, and hot soup we are going to enjoy for dinner," she coaxed, raising her voice to be heard. "That should keep your thoughts off of this uncomfortable, endless journey."

"How do you know what they be serving for the meal tonight?"

She grimaced as the carriage creaked, rocking to one side with a nasty lurch. "I do not know. It is something I wished for ever since the rain started."

"Hey! Whoa!" the driver John yelled. His panicked voice sounded over the clamor of the lashing rain. The carriage teetered momentarily before coming to a sudden stop. The communicating panel on the roof was thrust open. Only the coachman's eyes were visible on his muffled face. "My lady, there is a man lying down across the middle of the road. I think he's knocked his head. It looks like his leg is broke as well."

Before she could form an answer to this astonishing news, the sound of a horse's neigh reached her ears, and someone shouted. She came to her feet directly underneath the open panel. "What is happening?"

"Peter has the gentleman's horse, my lady. It appears he came to grief when he fell from his saddle.

One of his boots is caught in the stirrup," he bellowed over the roar of the storm.

"My lady! Your gown is getting soaked!" Josephine called out, gasping as she pointed at the stream of rainwater pouring inside the coach from the opened hatch.

She hastily closed the panel, moving away from the puddle of water on the floor, while wiping at the moisture collecting on her garment. She attempted to access the desperate situation they were in, while at the same time deciding what should be done. As Sophia pondered the problem, she quickly comprehended the most sensible decision. They certainly couldn't leave the injured gentleman on the ground, alone and helpless in a raging storm. She thrust the hatch open again, calling out to John, "We must bring the man with us to my aunt's home. I will make room in the carriage. Can he be moved with a broken limb?"

"No, my lady, it needs to be set. I can do it. I attended many gents with breaks to their legs during the war. I need to locate a couple of stout branches to use as a brace. Let me pull over. Peter and I will see to it." John shut the panel.

"My lady, no!" her maid exclaimed, putting a shaking hand to her forehead. "You can't be takin' up a stranger. We're very close to the Bath Road. He could be a highwayman!"

"I am not going to drive on, leaving a defenseless, wounded man lying in the road in pouring rain!" She sighed, dabbing at the wet spot on her gown before covering a puddle of water on the seat with the edge of her scarf. "I wish this storm would move on."

Josephine sat in disapproving silence, huddled

under the blanket. Sophia clutched her hands together while she tapped her booted feet on the floor in a nervous, repetitive movement as she listened to the muffled words and shouts from her coachman and groom outside. Then the carriage door banged open.

"My lady, we located two stout branches to use as a support, but I require somethin' else to secure them." The coachman wiped at his face with a sodden handkerchief. Water pooled on the rim of his hat before cascading over the edge to splash onto his coat.

She deliberated on something in her bag that might be of use. The answer suddenly came to her-the rolls of cloth she cut into small pieces to be used to apply her face lotion. "I brought several long strips of material. They are here in my case. Will that do?"

"Yes, my lady, it should do the trick."

John waited at the door while she rummaged for the cloth. She reached for two rolls bunched together at the bottom of her bag. "Here they are."

Without speaking, the coachman grabbed the material out of her hands and thumped the door shut.

"My lady, cover yourself with the blanket. You'll catch your death in this weather!"

"I am fine." She couldn't imagine lounging against the seat meekly waiting for the situation to resolve itself. Instead, she stood up, pacing back and forth on the tiny floor space inside the carriage. Several more nerve-racking, suspenseful minutes passed. She wished she could go outside and help the others. It was extremely frustrating to be cooped inside doing nothing.

"My lady, open up!" came John's muffled shout.

She grasped the knob, pushing the door wide open. The two men walked toward her with the injured man's arms draped across their shoulders. His head lolled to one side and then flopped forward against his chest. The lower half of his body was cradled in a rudimentary device, a burlap sack shaped into a makeshift cot.

"Stand over here next to me. If we loop our hands under his arms, we should be able to drag him inside," she instructed Josephine, as she crouched in the doorway.

With her maid's help, as well as the fortitude of John and Peter, the gentleman soon lay inert on his back on the floor of the carriage, wedged between the two seats.

"We'll get there as soon as possible, my lady!" shouted her coachman before he slammed the door closed once more.

Her maid resumed her place on the bench while Sophia maneuvered herself past the man's lifeless form, to crouch at a spot on the floor near his head. She glanced at his injured leg, braced with two branches, and bound together with the strips of cloth. She studied his torn breeches, his bare, muscular thigh exposed to her intent gaze. Her heart suddenly raced inside of her chest, leaving her with a breathless sensation. Chiding herself for being silly, reacting to the sight of uncovered skin in such a fashion, Sophia took a deep breath and looked away to inspect the gentleman's face. She stripped off her gloves and grasped the seat with one hand to steady herself as the coach heaved forward. With the storm continuing to rage outside, little daylight penetrated the inside of the vehicle. She could make out full lips over a firm chin, a blunt, commanding nose, and tousled, dark hair falling over the man's closed eyes.

She retrieved her damp scarf, folding it into a small mound of material, pushing the soft fabric underneath the gentleman's neck. Cradling his skull with her hand, she threaded her fingers through his dripping wet, silky locks, easing the tousled strands off his forehead.

"Uh! No!" the man grunted. He attempted to rise but fell back down with a groan, taking several deep, ragged breaths. The thick eyelashes framing his eyelids suddenly fluttered and opened wide.

Sophia gazed into a pair of well-remembered piercing green eyes. "Sir Edward!"

"I…It's you!" he muttered. "Wh…what…?"

"Shhh. It is best not to attempt to speak." She tried to shift to a more comfortable position, but he winced at the sudden movement. She held herself as still as possible. "I will tell you what little I know."

"My lady! Whatever are you about?" Josephine sat up in a rigid posture, staring at her.

"Do not be concerned." Sophia twisted around, frowning at her maid. "The gentleman and I are acquainted. I am explaining as best I can what happened."

"Your…your despotic companion?" he queried, with a weak chuckle.

"Thankfully, no," she countered. "Merely my fretful lady's maid."

"Ah." He sighed. "A singular individual in a position to be only slightly less irritating."

"Indeed." She moved one hand away from his head to grip his shoulder. "Now please, be quiet and listen to me. You must conserve your strength."

"I am yours to command," he uttered before groaning, closing his eyes as the coach suddenly lurched.

She held onto him, bracing as best she could against further jostling. "You cultivate the art of flirtation even at the height of agony and affliction? Admirable!"

His chest rose underneath her hand as he took a deep breath. "I...It is imperative to stay steadfast to my chosen guise or countenance, if you will agree."

"No. At this moment, I cannot concur with you. You are being ridiculous, in your present state, to spend even a moments' thought on such a trivial matter." She bent over to whisper in his ear. "Listen to me. You fell off your horse. There is a bump the size of a goose egg on the back of your head. You were insensible when we came upon you. Your leg is broken. It must have been wrenched before you fell when your foot became stuck. We located your boot in the stirrup. John, my coachman, and a batman during the war, set your leg before we moved you."

He exhaled deeply again. "I trust the procedure was done properly?"

"He assured me he was called upon to perform the duty many times on the battlefield," she apprised him, hoping she sounded confident.

"My horse?" He opened his eyes to stare at her with penetrating directness.

She frowned, going over the discussions she heard and the actions she observed since his discovery. "I believe the animal did not suffer any grave injury. My coachman made no mention of it. I had no chance to inquire while I made certain your leg was protected from further harm. My groom Peter should be riding him."

He grunted. "I hope you are correct. Where are we headed?"

"I am taking you to my destination, South Hill Park Mansion in Bracknell, Berkshire. My aunt, Mrs. Joan Canning resides there," she replied.

He didn't speak for a moment. "Canning. Is…is she any relation to Mr. George Canning?"

She smiled. "Yes, she is married to him. He is my uncle."

He stared at her. "You left London and plan on rusticating in Berkshire at your aunt's home before the season is over? What happened?"

She pursed her lips together, looking away before turning back to glare at him. "Nothing at all. I am visiting my extended family."

"I do not believe you." His eyebrows came together in one dark line. "I'm confused."

She rubbed his shoulder. "Of course, you are. You whacked your head."

He scowled. "No. My noggin is sore, but I am alert. I am perplexed by you."

Taken aback by his comment, she uttered, "By…by me?"

"Yes. You have no resemblance to the Lady Sophia Hampton I met last summer. The lady invited to spend several days at my estate for a summer house party thought of no one but herself the entire time. That woman would be in hysterics at this moment, if not already succumbing to a fit of the vapors."

She attempted a lighthearted giggle; it came out as a tremorous squawk. "Nonsense! I simply reacted in concern to someone who suffered a serious injury."

He glared at her. "I don't know what kind of rig

you are playing at, but you will not stop me from getting to the reason for your deception as soon as I am able."

Chapter Three

Her exquisite violet-hued eyes widened. She released her hold on his shirt. "Deception? I…I do not understand you. You…you are more grievously hurt than I first supposed."

"It is too late to play the silly, coy miss with me," he muttered, closing his eyes as the coach came to a sudden, swaying stop jarring him. "Either we arrived at your destination, or we are stuck in the mud on the road in the middle of nowhere."

She gripped the edge of the seat, slowly standing up, rubbing her cold hands across her skirt. "For your sake, I hope we are at South Hill Park."

"You are frozen. You will certainly be sick, my lady." Her maid shook one gloved finger at her. "I did warn you."

The coach door flew open. "We made it, my lady. The storm let up, only a light mist be fallin'."

"Thank goodness. Josephine, come with me. I need to greet my aunt and tell her of our injured passenger." She turned to look at him. "I will endeavor to inquire about a bedchamber and request a surgeon be called as soon as possible. The footmen will assist John and Peter with your removal from the coach."

"I am forever in your debt," he muttered, gazing at her until she stepped outside. He struggled to rise on his elbow and called out, "Which of you is Peter?"

"I am, uh…sir." A bedraggled, ruddy-faced lad with a wet, muddied cap on his thick red hair stood at the door of the coach.

"My…my horse," he paused, taking a deep breath as a jolt of sharp pain shot through his leg. "How is he?"

"No harm done, sir." The boy stopped speaking to doff his hat. "A prime un if I say so myself."

"Beg your pardon, sir." Another, older, taller man with a sodden, drooping scarf wrapped around his throat appeared in the doorway. "I checked your horse after we loaded you into the coach and observed his gait while Peter rode him. He is in fine shape. Just wet, tired, and hungry. The lads took him to the stables. They will look after him."

"Am I addressing John?" he grunted the query.

"Yes, sir." The man thrust his chin out, placing his hands on his hips.

"I understand you served as a batman during the recent wars. You set various broken limbs. Tell me exactly what you did to my leg."

John lowered his arms to his sides, clearing his throat before speaking. "The break is a clean un, sir, in the shin area. The bone went back in place quite easily. Peter and I secured it with a pair of sturdy branches. Lady Sophia gave me some strapping material to bind it with. Sorry about your breeches. I couldn't properly attend to the injury without tearing them open."

"No matter. I trust it will heal without requiring adjustment." He shivered before closing his eyes, slowly lying back down on the floor. The many hours prone and insensible on the road in pouring rain could cause serious consequences. It was ludicrous to be concerned about his leg when debilitating fevers meant almost certain death.

****

Sophia dipped the cloth in the bowl of cool lavender water once again before squeezing out the excess liquid. Leaning across the bed, she wiped his hot forehead and flushed cheeks, now covered with several days' growth of beard. Her hands moved in a gentle, soothing motion across his face. She studied his unresponsive countenance, as he lay still and fixed against the pillow. His injured leg had been examined soon after they arrived. The local surgeon gave his own worthy opinion the bone was set as well as he could do himself. He replaced the haphazard brace of broken branches, with pieces of finely cut wood and wrapped the limb with clean bandages made from torn sheets before propping it up on top of a sturdy wooden crate. A blanket tossed across Sir Edward's lower body covered his exposed thigh. Insensible when the men lifted him out of the coach, he had remained so for three succeeding nights. It was just after dawn on the fourth day.

"Come now, you must get well," she whispered in his ear. "You vowed to solve my little mystery. At first, I was alarmed by your intimidation but after a period of deliberation, I am now quite eager to participate in your challenge. The years spent adopting this role has given me a decided advantage. I see no harm in continuing to confuse you with my pretense."

"Has he come around, my dear?"

Sophia stood up and hastily moved away from the bed. "No...no, Aunt, there isn't any change."

"You must be exhausted," the lady observed, as

she walked inside the room to stand next to her. "You have scarcely left Sir Edward's side since they bought him in."

She dropped the cloth into the bowl, gripping her aunt's arm, leading her out into the hallway. "I implore you, when he does wake up, please do not mention my frequent presence in his bedchamber."

The older woman's brown eyes twinkled as she reached up to straighten the frivolous cap, perched on her head to a jaunty angle on top of her golden-brown curls. "You have no wish to receive his gratitude? Very well, I will be as mum as a statue on the subject. You believe his fever is about to break?"

She glanced back at the still figure on the bed and sighed. "I sense he is not as warm as he was yesterday."

"Well, that is a good sign, isn't it?" Aunt Joan patted her hand. "I am off to the kitchen to see Cook to discuss the day's meals. I received a letter from your uncle yesterday and must send a reply. See that you rest later today."

"I will," she promised as she watched her walk away toward the back stairs. Since her arrival, Sophia had observed Aunt Joan's calm, composed attitude to the current stressful situation. Three of her four cousins were away at school. But Charles, the youngest, was still at home, and usually up to some sort of mischief. Her aunt had a busy household to oversee as well as an illustrious husband in the government. He valued her thoughts and opinions concerning nagging issues that came before him at his post in London. Two letters had arrived from him in the scope of three days. Even the unlooked-for presence of an injured stranger in her home failed to discompose the lady. She took the matter in stride, happy to be able to offer a room and a clean bed for Sir Edward to recuperate in.

"Lady Sophia, how is our patient today?" A man's voice interrupted her thoughts.

She started in surprise, turning around to find Mr. Gordon, standing in front of her holding his bag. "I am…sorry. I was woolgathering. I am hopeful he has improved."

"I am very relieved to hear that." He followed her into the room. "If Sir Edward is better, he almost certainly owes his life to you."

"I wish to speak to you of that very matter," she paused, to stare at the inert form in the bed before taking a deep breath. "If he has indeed turned the corner and begun to rally, please do not mention my role in his recovery when you do speak with him."

The surgeon's thick eyebrows lowered over his eyes. "Why do you not wish the gentleman to know of your courtesy to him?"

She shrugged her shoulders, grimacing. "Call it maidenly modesty or a silly notion of mine. I find it a daunting image, an unmarried man indebted to me."

He frowned at her. "I am sure you are aware, my lady, society's strict rules of supervision for young women are overlooked in the sickroom, especially when the patient is senseless and unresponsive."

"You do not understand. I will be completely frank." She clasped her hands together in front of her, staring directly at the surgeon. "I refuse to be obligated to marry any man whether I know him from a London ball, a house party in the country or upon a sick bed in my aunt's home."

His brows rose when she finished speaking. "As

you wish, my lady. However, I believe you are doing yourself a disservice. I promise not to bring up the subject. Now, excuse me, I must examine my patient."

With a backward glance at the motionless shape on the bed, she walked out of the room and headed down the hall for the kitchen garden. The day after she arrived, the weather cleared long enough for her to take a stroll on a pathway leading to some dense woods behind the house. On her return, her boots became very muddy. Not wanting to dirty the main entrance, she followed the cobblestone path taking her to the back door. Just before she reached the enclosed herb garden, she noticed what appeared to be a tiny cottage half hidden behind some overgrown shrubs. Intrigued, she made her way around the dense foliage to the front of the structure. She observed two small windows on either side of a partially open door. It was swinging back and forth in the light breeze while the hinges creaked in a steady, mournful rhythm.

She strode up the lopsided steps, slowly pushing the door wide open. "Hello?"

"Yes, miss?" An elderly man with a lined, wrinkled face wearing a dirt-stained smock over dark brown breeches and a faded green shirt, looked up at her from a workbench. "Can I be of some assistance?"

She noticed his hands were covered in dirt. Some pots with seeds were arranged on the table in front of him. "I didn't mean to disturb your work. Are you the gardener?"

"Yes." He rubbed his hands together, shaking off some of the soil before taking off his hat and straightening to face her. "I be Ned Grimmer, head groundskeeper at South Hill Park. I be planting seedlings of a particular jasmine plant Mrs. Canning favors."

"I am her niece, Lady Sophia Hampton." She smiled at the man and then studied the interior of the shed. Three of the walls were lined with rough, wooden countertops. In the center, there was a small sink. All the surfaces were relatively clean except for the table where Mr. Grimmer worked. "I am staying here with my aunt for an extended period and find myself confronted with a dilemma. I create face lotion used by many ladies of fashion in London and require the mixture to be placed inside small, glass vials before they are sent to town. This is best accomplished in a place away from the main house. Do you suppose I could use a bit of counter space here to mix my solution?"

The man's eyebrows furrowed across his lined forehead. "Face lotion, my lady? You don't need a stove for your concoction?"

"No, no," she hastened to reassure him. "I soak rice flour in lemon juice, grind it into a paste and then blend in olive oil at the end of the process for a smooth texture. I will put down parchment to make sure the table where I work is not stained."

"I see no problem with you doing that here." He frowned. "Is Mrs. Canning aware of what you are up to?"

She felt her face flush as she smiled at the man. "No, and I do not plan to tell her. As you may imagine, it is hard for women of my class to understand a lady's wish to dabble in commerce. My servants are aware of my endeavors. They will make certain the packed bottles reach town and are loaded on the mail coach heading to London."

"I'm not going to say anything against you takin' a place here. But I worry your aunt does not comprehend what you are doin'."

"I am firm in my wish she is not to be told." She stared at him. "How does my request sit with you, Mr. Grimmer?"

He sighed. "Very well, my lady, I won't say any more about it."

The crotchety old man was still concerned about the possibility of his mistress discovering her secret pastime. He probably assumed he merited punishment if his master or mistress learned of the enterprise.

"I assure you if my aunt should discover my ruse, no fault will be attached to you."

The gardener grunted a reply before turning back to the seedlings.

She quickly gathered and carried her supplies into the cottage under his watchful, apprehensive gaze. The day before, she managed to soak a good amount of rice in lemon juice. Today, she planned to grind the softened kernels into a paste and then blend in the olive oil before pouring the face lotion into the glass containers. She learned the mail coach stopped in the nearby village on its return to London. Josephine could notify John when the vials were ready. It was a simple matter for him to see the crate safely installed on the vehicle headed back to the city.

She had finished pouring the last of her concoction into a vial when the door to the cottage burst open. Her maid strode into the room.

"Mrs. Canning is asking for you, my lady. I..." Josephine abruptly stopped speaking when the gardener followed her inside.

Sophia smiled when she observed her maid's hesitation. "Mr. Grimmer knows of my project and wish to keep the details from my aunt. You can discuss it in his presence without worry."

"Very well." Josephine cleared her throat and bobbed a curtsey to the man, "How do you do?"

Mr. Grimmer nodded to her before turning away to bend over his workbench.

"What did you say to my aunt?" She wedged the last glass container inside the crate, carefully closing the lid before dipping her goose quill pen into ink and writing the direction of the chemist's shop in the city on the top.

Her maid pursed her lips and frowned before replying. "I told her you were just waking up from a nap. She requested you join her as soon as possible in the patient's room. The gentleman is awake."

"Oh, indeed. That is very good news!" She started to walk toward the door but then stopped and pulled her watch out of her pocket. Nine thirty already. "See that John takes the crate to the posting house in town without delay. The mail coach leaves at eleven for London."

Josephine raised her brows. "Yes, my lady. But shouldn't I return with you to your chamber to assist you?"

"No, thank you." She put her hands behind her back to untie the straps on the apron she wore to protect her gown. She lifted it over her head, tossing it onto the counter. "It is a simple matter to splash some water on my face and redo my hair. I will see you before dinner."

She strode out of the door, down the steps, heading

for the back entrance to the house. She located the servant's staircase on the first day, tucked away in a corner, leading to their rooms on the upper floors. It served nicely for her purpose of going in and out of the house without being observed by her aunt.

Sophia reached her room without mishap, quickly completing her ablutions. Admittedly a little late in the day, but it was time to decide how she should handle an awake and alert Sir Edward. It had been a simple matter to see to him while delirious. The male servants in her aunt's household would now be required to assist him. She sent a note to his mother and sister two days ago. It would not be surprising if they arrived here today or tomorrow with his valet in tow. She studied her reflection in the mirror, as she combed and secured her hair in a tight bun at the back of her head. Sir Edward and his family needed to decide the type of care he should receive, from this point forward, to best ensure a full recovery. With this weighty matter solved, she patted one wayward curl that fell over her ear and picked up her shawl from the end of the bed before stepping out into the hallway, ready to confront the patient.

Chapter Four

He heard footsteps. A shuffling followed by no sound at all. The sudden quiet contained an eerie quality. The noiselessness caused him to feel deserted. He became aware of a negligible noise, a tip tapping, tip tapping as if someone walked on their toes instead of using their whole foot, then the stillness again.

He attempted to study the surroundings, but he made out only a pinkish-colored haze. Could there be something covering his eyes? He summoned the strength to force his chin to move to the right and to the left. Nothing changed.

He took a deep breath endeavoring to bring order to his tumultuous thoughts, despite searing pain brought on by the sensation of an assortment of at least ten blacksmiths pounding hammers inside his head. He tried to acknowledge his perceptions. He believed his current dwelling was a room. Was he standing or sitting? He thrust his head backward, feeling support at his neck. He reached up with one trembling hand to clutch soft material at his shoulder and froze. *Could he be lying in a bed?*

"W…Where?" He struggled to push the word across his shriveled tongue and through his dry, cracked lips. The inside of his mouth was dry as dust. He had never felt so parched.

He lifted his upper body, attempting to pull himself

to a sitting position. As he did so, he ascertained the dimness affecting his eyesight was the inside of his eyelids. They were tightly closed. He sensed they had held that position for quite some time. He gritted his teeth, forcing them open.

He blinked. A tall, silver goblet sat next to a water pitcher on a bedside table. Without further consideration, he moved his hand forward in one swift, jerking motion toward the vessel. He felt a greedy desperation in that moment, not unlike what the lone traveler surely experienced in the middle of a sweltering hot, dry desert when spotting a mirage.

He managed to grasp the goblet but as he lifted it, his arm quivered. It slipped through his fingers to land with a loud clatter to the floor. "Damn!"

The door to the chamber burst open. A young lad of about seven summers barged into the room. "I heard a noise."

He grimaced as he pointed at the mess. "I am sorry. I attempted to take a drink. I couldn't get a grip."

"Let me help you, sir." The boy retrieved the container from the floor, pouring water from the pitcher before holding it out to him.

"I am weak as a babe!" he exclaimed as the liquid sloshed over the rim. The lad reached out to clutch his hand. He continued to shake, spilling water all over his shirt. He managed to obtain a few sips before lying back against the pillow. "Thank…Thank you."

"You are welcome." The boy put the goblet back on the table before looking up at him, frowning. "I checked on you every day. At first, you didn't move. The next morning you moaned. The following day you were thrashing and pulling at the bedclothes something fierce. Your face turned red. You were sweating. I became worried. My mother told me you were in the throes of a temp...tempestuous fever. Yesterday you quieted down somewhat. The surgeon checked on you. He told us you were much improved. I never expected you couldn't hold a glass when you woke up."

He managed to grin at the lad before turning away to gaze at his surroundings. "How long....? What the...my leg!"

"It is broken."

He took several deep breaths, attempting to calm his racing pulse as he studied his bound limb and the contraption it rested on. "I vaguely recall...Tell me, boy...What is your name, by the way?"

"It is Charles, sir."

"Charles, do you know, has the surgeon been here recently?" he questioned with a scowl, as he attempted to remember how he came to be in his current, grievous state.

"Um..." The lad gazed at the ceiling. "He visited last evening. I came to look in on you. Mama stood at the door talking to him. She told me to return to the nursery to eat my supper."

"Could you tell me where I am?" He groaned as a shaft of pain tore through his leg. "What is your mother's name?"

"You are at South Hill Park, sir," Charles answered with pride. "It is in Bracknell, Berkshire. My mother is Mrs. Canning."

"Canning...I recall...Berkshire...most probably on my way home..." he stopped speaking as the sound of more footsteps reverberated in the hall.

A short, buxom woman wearing a white apron over

her gown with a lacey cap on top of her head, covering most of her golden, brown curls entered the room. "Charles, I hope you didn't tire out our injured guest with your ceaseless chatter."

"Not at all, ma'am," Edward spoke out. "He has been a great help to me. Without his assistance I never could have managed to drink some water."

"Did you hear that, Mother?" Charles piped up. "I am not bothersome."

"Good boy." She lovingly tousled his hair as she smiled at Edward. "I am very happy to see you awake and talking."

"You must be the lady of the house." He offered her his fingers with a shaking hand. "I want to express my deepest thanks."

She chuckled as she clutched his hand. "I am sorry to be so informal and not introduce myself. I am Mrs. Canning. I assume my son has already told you his name."

"Yes, he has. He also informed me he kept a close watch on my condition for the past few days." He paused as he noticed a bowl of water and a cloth dropped beside it on the table. "Are you the one I should be grateful to for wiping my heated brow while in the depths of fever, Charles?"

"No, sir. It…"

"Charles, enough talking now," Mrs. Canning interrupted. "Go to the nursery and drink your tea."

"Yes, Mother. Good-bye, sir." The lad bobbed his head to him before shuffling out of the room.

"I am sorry, Mrs. Canning." Edward chewed on his lower lip in consternation before grinning at her. "I didn't mean to put anyone in an uncomfortable position by mentioning the consideration given to me while I was delirious. Is there a daughter, other sons living here, or perhaps you tended me?"

The lady clasped her hands together, not speaking for a moment. "My daughter and two other sons are all away at school…"

"What do I see? My patient is awake and talking? Wonderful!" A rotund, older gentleman with a thatch of gray hair covering the crown of his head, entered the room. He carried a black bag.

Mrs. Canning took a deep breath, looking noticeably relieved by the man's sudden entrance. "This is the surgeon, Mr. Gordon, Sir Edward. He has attended to you since you arrived four days ago. I will leave you two to discuss the situation. I need to check on the dinner preparations."

"Nothing more than gruel and a thin slice of bread for my patient this evening."

The lady paused on the threshold. "Of course, I will inform Cook."

"Gruel?" Edward grimaced at him.

The man cleared his throat as he dropped his bag to the floor. "I cannot allow you to eat meats, or potatoes and heavy gravies at present. Those foods could cause serious pain if ingested in an empty stomach."

"With the abundance of hunger pains I am experiencing at present, I can't imagine a piece of vegetable or a bit of beef would be a problem," he replied, in a beguiling manner.

"You might be surprised. Take it slowly. You will be eating hearty food in no time." The surgeon picked up a pillow from off the floor before going to the foot of the bed. He grasped the crate with one hand, gently removing it from under the bandaged foot, securing the pillow there instead. "There is no need for this apparatus now that the fever has broken. I used it as a precaution to keep your leg as stabilized as possible while you were delirious and thrashing around. You will be more comfortable without it."

Edward couldn't contain a gasp as the surgeon lowered his foot. "I am stiff as a board."

"That is to be expected. However, the best thing you can do is to lie and rest. Let Mrs. Canning and her servants take care of all your needs in the meantime."

He frowned at the man. "Be frank with me. Will my leg heal properly? As I vaguely recall, a coachman of uncertain reputation set the bone at the scene of my accident."

The surgeon glared down at him with raised brows. "I can assure you, sir, the loyal men who serve as batmen during the wars apprehend as much as medical men do about the process and the proper methods of setting broken bones from repetitive practice on the battlefields. They are as proficient at the task as we are. You were most fortunate John arrived on the scene shortly after you were injured. Provided you stay off your feet for seven to ten days, you will be able to get around with a cane initially. After a few more weeks you should walk normally and resume your usual activities."

"As long as that?" He made a mental note to offer the coachman his profound gratitude.

Mr. Gordon pursed his lips together and gazed intently at him before answering his query in a grave manner. "Yes, you must keep as still as possible for the next several days if the bone is to set correctly."

He scowled at the thought of forced inactivity for so long a time and the need to rely on others to help him with personal cleanliness. He looked away to hide the frustration he felt, again noticing the cloth and empty bowl on the bedside table. "What of my fever? I understand I stayed delirious and unresponsive for four days. Are you the one to thank for mopping my brow?"

The surgeon cleared his throat. "I…"

"Greetings, Mr. Gordon. Is it true the patient's fever has broken?" a woman's cheery voice sounded from out in the hallway. "Oh, hello there."

He gripped the bed sheets, gaping as Lady Sophia entered the room. "It is you! I didn't remember."

"I…I need to make other calls. I will return tomorrow," the surgeon blurted the words as he reached for his bag, striding out of the room.

"Tsk, tsk! Quite a blow to my self-esteem to have made such a negligible impression on you." She walked to the window, standing with her back to him.

"Ha! I remember enough of our previous conversation to tell you that ploy won't work with me any longer." He frowned at her backside. "Turn around and explain yourself."

She faced him with a silly grin on her face. "What do you wish for me to decipher? Is it so shocking I am preoccupied with my appearance?"

"I have warned you, I comprehended your game," he bellowed at her in frustration. "Stop it! Be honest with me."

She looked away from him, staring at the open door. "Shhh! The others will hear you. They will assume you are in pain."

"I am not going to deny you exasperate me." He

winced. "It is not far off the mark to say I feel a headache coming on."

"You have no one but yourself to blame if your head is sore," she countered, folding her arms across her chest.

"Indeed?" He glared at her with one eyebrow cocked. "How do you come to surmise such a thing?"

"Whatever were you thinking? You took your horse out in one of the worst storms of the year!" She scowled at him. "If my coachman had failed to spot you and obtained my permission to stop and pick you up, the consequences of your harebrained decision would have been much worse."

"Do not forget my complexion. No doubt it suffered irreplaceable damage as well!" he goaded her. "You needn't scold. I will remind you the rainstorm came out of nowhere, with no warning."

"I admonish you? I'm rapidly losing all patience with you, sir."

"And I with you," he grumbled, gripping the sheets. "The surgeon informed me I will be tied to this bed for a period of seven to ten days. How do you propose we go on?"

She stared at him with her glorious violet-hued eyes glimmering. She made a huffing sound before speaking. "Well, I suppose we must agree to appear at least outwardly congenial to each other."

"I see," he replied, intently studying her expression. "And inside, what are we actually thinking?"

"I…I am not decided."

He snorted. "Let me know when the answer comes to you."

She lifted her chin, glaring at him. "I doubt if there will be any reason to speak with you in the coming days."

"You won't be able to help yourself," he responded, with conviction. "Unlike the situation at my house party last summer when there were multiple people to converse with, I comprehend only your aunt and nephew are in residence here."

"Your confidence is misplaced, sir." She turned away, walking toward the open door.

He chuckled. "If only you were a betting man…"

She gasped, twisting around, glaring at him. "What are you implying?"

"You cannot deny how much simpler it would be to spend time here alone with me if you were a man." He grimaced. "It pains me to admit, the entire dismal situation I find myself in is much more tolerable with your presence here."

She studied him with raised brows before moving once again toward the door. "I suppose I should be grateful for that backhanded compliment."

"By the way, before you leave, I wish to thank you," he called out.

She turned to face him again. "Thank me? Whatever for?"

He grinned. "Why, for diligently wiping my brow during the height of the fever, of course."

Chapter Five

"Hello, my dear." Aunt Joan walked toward her with a smile on her face as Sophia made her way down the hall, away from Sir Edward's chamber. "I hope you feel much better after your rest."

"Re…? Oh, yes, of course." She cleared her throat before continuing. "I am much improved."

Her aunt put a hand on her arm, leading her to the front entry. "I know how exhausting the sickroom can be. With four children to watch over, at least one of them is usually indisposed."

"I cannot imagine how you do everything, taking care of my niece and nephews, discussing meals with Cook, ensuring the continued upkeep of the house, the stables and grounds, as well as maintaining your diligent correspondence with my uncle," she told her.

"It is easier now, with the three older children away at school," Aunt Joan clarified.

"I am certain your days are very busy with other tasks even when they are gone," she acknowledged.

Her aunt nodded to the butler Hendrik as he opened the door to the drawing room. She led the way inside to two chairs flanking a roaring fire. "Please sit down, my dear. Our tea will arrive momentarily. There are many responsibilities and tasks to fulfill but the work is a joy when it is done for a family you love and cherish. Did your maid give you my message? I believe you saw Sir

Edward?"

"Yes, she did," Sophia replied. "And yes, I did visit him."

"How did you find our patient?" she queried with a smile. "He appears to be much better."

"Yes…yes he is." She deliberately gave a vague answer, vowing to think on what she discussed with him later in the privacy of her bedchamber.

"It is a tremendous relief the fever has finally broken," the other lady observed. "Thank goodness your uncle is rarely ill."

Sophia studied her aunt's lopsided grin and the faraway look in her eyes. "You are a lucky woman to be married to such a devoted husband. Will you please tell me how you met my uncle?"

A knock sounded on the door. A footman entered the room. A kitchen maid followed behind him carrying a tray. After placing the refreshments on the table in front of their mistress and inquiring if she required anything else, the two servants bowed and left the room.

"Of course." Her aunt poured the tea before handing her a cup. "I must admit no fireworks exploded when I first met George in seventeen ninety-nine. It was certainly not love at first sight."

Sophia placed her cup in the saucer while she waited for the beverage to cool. "You surprise me."

"Please help yourself." Aunt Joan pointed to the plates of tiny cucumber sandwiches and lemon tarts. "You will be astounded when I tell you the Princess of Wales revealed her attraction to him just before we were formally introduced."

In the act of putting her teacup to her lips when her

aunt made the startling observation, she left the cup suspended in air. "The princess?"

"Yes, indeed." Aunt Joan placed a sandwich on the edge of her saucer before continuing. "They were close acquaintances initially. On one of his visits to see her, the two of them were alone for a few minutes. She made an advance to him that made it obvious she wished for their relationship to go beyond friendship."

Sophia put her cup back down in the saucer and tried to imagine her uncle in such a position. "Did he return her interest?"

"He told me he felt flattered at first but soon came to the conclusion she had placed him in an extremely delicate situation." She took a sip of her tea. "He wrote to his good friend Lord Granville asking for advice. While deciding how he should manage the predicament, he visited Walmer Castle near Dover as a guest of Mr. Pitt. I took a sojourn there with my guardian and kinsman Viscount Dundas and his wife Lady Jane at the same time."

Sophia grinned. "How very romantic to become acquainted in a castle!"

Aunt Joan laughed. "I hate to disappoint you, dear. George purposely avoided me for the first several days of his sojourn there."

"What?" She hastily swallowed piece of tart, patting her lips with a serviette. "How could such a thing happen?"

"Well, as he explained to me many months later," her aunt paused, gazing dreamily down into her teacup, "due to the unpleasant circumstance with the princess, he initially wanted nothing to do with female companionship while at Walmer. He didn't even bother to learn my identity until the second day of his visit. Then he associated me as *Miss Scott, a particular friend of Lady Jane.* He also recalled hearing my name coupled with another gentleman, who I had intended to marry. After a subsequent proposal, he understood I refused my suitor. He determined I should be avoided at all costs, thinking the last thing he needed at that time was idle gossip linked to his name. The company at the castle proved large enough to allow him to contrive to refrain from sitting next to me at dinner as well. He managed to give every one of the officers from the Fleet and Army, who were in attendance, the seat at my side for the next ten days."

Sophia giggled. "He sounds pompous as well as brash."

"That was my impression at first," her aunt concurred. "But suddenly, with his chaise ready and waiting at the door, he didn't wish to go away without a chance to further his acquaintance with me. He applied to my guardian for leave to stay another day."

Sophia raised her brows in surprise. "I never expected to hear you say that."

"I felt bewildered as well." Her aunt placed her empty cup down onto the saucer. "He spent most of the time by my side the next day, but he made no real effort to speak to me or to offer any sort of admission of the true state of his feelings. He explained later he suffered from extreme embarrassment and remorse. He put himself in an uncomfortable circumstance, not being quite certain of the emotions he felt toward me. He believed the situation would most likely lead to a refusal on my part if he made a declaration at the time."

"I can imagine. Certainly, a very awkward position

for him to be in." Sophia put her plate on the table. "Did he say anything specific to you before he left?"

"Yes. He lingered until early afternoon. He informed me afterward, he had hoped to be able to find a time to engage in a private conversation but failed to secure the opportunity." She sighed. "George returned to Walmer two weeks later to spend a fortnight there. We were able to become better acquainted at that time. He did apply to my brother-in-law, your uncle by marriage, the Marquess of Titchfield for permission to marry me. Uncertain about giving his approval, the Marquess withheld his agreement to our union. I abided by his wishes at first."

"You believed you did not love my uncle?"

"No, I certainly cared for him." After a short pause, she continued the conversation, "It proved a matter of trust as well as a great life change for me. As you are aware, my father, your grandfather, left a great deal of money to me and my sisters when he passed away three months before my birth. I did not wish to be married for my money. George, while certainly a prosperous government official, could never hope to make the kind of funds I brought to the match. If I married him, an opportunity would be lost to connect myself with a peer of the realm, and I would become nothing more than the wife of a man of high authority in government, who spent most of his time in the city. I believed those circumstances were not conducive to a happy married life."

"I admire you, Aunt. Marriage and happiness. Those two words are rarely coupled together in one sentence to my knowledge. I am told it is a woman's duty to join together in wedlock with a titled man so he may gain heirs, thereby furthering his lineage, continuing to keep the properties and funds within the rightful family coffers. In return, the women are expected to give up all possessions as well as limited independence to daily subservience of their husband. You thought of yourself and your own need for a content, happy life as you pondered whether you wished to marry."

"You are correct, my dear. Happiness is something I greatly value, much more than the actual institution of marriage itself." She paused. "I continued to be uncertain for several months. I decided to visit my guardian Lord Dundas and his wife at their home in Wimbledon. I quickly learned he and Lady Jane approved of Mr. Canning as a suitor. George became a regular visitor there. However, in April I received a summons to London from my sister and brother-in-law. Lord Titchfield still withheld his consent to my marriage and all visits from George ceased at that time."

"I imagine you grew closer to him during your stay in Wimbledon. It must have been extremely hard to suddenly not see him at all."

"The course I set for myself proved onerous," her aunt agreed. "I resigned myself to follow what my brother-in-law believed was a progression for the best. However, a few weeks after my arrival in London, I contracted a chill while out walking in the park. I fell gravely ill for many days."

Sophia sat up straight against the cushions at her back. "Oh, my goodness. How terrible! I do not recall being aware of that."

"You were not yet two years old," Aunt Joan

pointed out, as she poured herself more tea. "Certainly, it was a harrowing period. Your mother left you with your nanny and came to help Henrietta nurse me. When the worst of my illness finally passed and I recovered, I suddenly comprehended the feelings in my heart. I loved George and wanted to marry him. William, Lord Titchfield, recognized my sincere emotions and withdrew his opposition to our union. We were married a month later on July the eighth, eighteen hundred."

"You did not waste a moment once you made your decision!" Sophia smiled wistfully, wiping at a bit of moisture around her eyes.

"When you understand, without question, the situation is right, there is no need to wait." Aunt Joan took a sip of her tea, gazing at her over the rim of her cup before placing it back in the saucer. "Sophia, you are almost twenty-one years old. It is past time you set up your own household. Did I detect a note of anger in your voice when you gave your opinion of society's expectations when women decide to marry? Surely the institution of family unions has not sunk so low in every case! Has no gentleman caught your fancy?"

"Yes, once." She stared at the patterns on the carpeted floor, allowing the memories to resurface buried in the back of her mind for so long. "I turned sixteen, too young to know better. He...he was the youngest son of an Earl. His family visited friends in the area close to my home. I walked early one morning...we met by chance. He joined me on my stroll...we spoke of nothings at first, the weather, the spring flowers. I quickly sensed an ease, a comfort with him. We embarked on discussing our hopes and dreams for the future. I...I felt a floodgate had opened. Both of us babbled and chattered, agreeing, and arguing over beliefs and opinions. It was so wonderful!"

"It sounds as if the two of you recognized an instant attraction," her aunt observed.

"I thought we did." She stopped for a moment, frowning in recollection. "I certainly believed something special occurred between us at the time. We continued to meet daily for over a week."

Aunt Joan studied her for a moment. "So, you experienced a brief, innocent friendship?"

"No. Not quite." She pondered the glowing embers in the fireplace wondering how much to tell her. "A…several days after we met, we stood on the shore of a pond engaged in a silly game of who could skip a rock the farthest. He claimed to win at five skips. I insisted I bested him with six. We laughed together over the nonsensical arguments we each put forth to prove our claims. He suddenly bent over and kissed me. I…I returned his embrace."

Her aunt sighed. "How many of us have been caught up in the throes of romantic attraction in our youth! I often thought it advantageous to be born with the innate knowledge of stolen kisses leading to dashed, impractical hopes when we are young. How painful it can be when those dreams are crushed! Perhaps it is better to learn those hard lessons for ourselves early in life. What happened, my dear?"

Sophia winced as she silently acknowledged her experience led to much more than an embrace. The motivation for what had happened was never far from her consciousness. She was in love and believed she would soon be married. "I went walking as usual the next morning. He never joined me. That evening, I had just finished dressing for dinner and heard a tap-tapping on my bedchamber window. I walked over to draw back the drapes and opened the sash. He stood directly below in the bushes. I can still hear his hoarse, agitated voice calling out to me. He told me his father needed to return to their estate. A severe rainstorm caused flooding in many of the tenant homes. They were leaving early in the morning. He…He thanked me for the enjoyable time we had together and turned away with a casual wave. I believed he planned to return before much time passed to speak to my father, but I never saw him again."

"I am sorry, Sophia, such a hard thing to face when you are young and impressionable." Her aunt frowned. "But surely there were other worthy gentlemen you were introduced to over the years?"

She took a deep breath, willing away the heavy ache in her heart before replying. "You use the word *worthy*, Aunt. Yes, I can attest to meeting several decent, respectable men in London. But I could never see myself married to any of them and guessed early on the only real interest they had was not for me but for my dowry. One gentleman did tell me I would *bring the epitome of grace and loveliness to the foot of his dining table*, other potential suitors exclaimed over the unusual color of my eyes or my thick, black hair. I managed to discourage them before they requested an audience with my father."

Her aunt studied her for a moment with her hands clasped tightly together in her lap. "I want to ask you something, my dear. I do not mean to pry, but I must confess I am confused. As you know, your mother and I correspond regularly. Her letters frequently bemoan *excessive preoccupation with your appearance.* She worries your habits may cause gentlemen who are attracted to you to become disinterested, to hold you in distain. I must say I observed no such absorption or distraction since you arrived here. Is this something you only concern yourself with while in London?"

She deliberated how many, if any of the details, she should give to her aunt. Along with her other fine qualities, the good lady proved extremely observant. It was probably best to be as honest as possible with her. She cleared her throat before speaking. "I mentioned I discouraged the gentlemen before they expressed an interest in me to my father…"

Her aunt's eyes widened, and she stared intently at her. "You don't mean…It cannot be an act?"

Sophia shrugged her shoulders, smiling ruefully. "It has served my purpose wonderfully. You are aware of the reason for my temporary banishment from London. An extremely unfortunate thing to happen at the Covington ball. I am thankful a formal announcement of Lord Dunson's betrothal appeared shortly before the incident in the papers. I could not be forced to marry him!"

"But this elaborate ruse…" She frowned. "Surely there were moments when you forgot to pretend?"

"Certainly, playing such a role can be exhausting. I developed a friendship with a gentleman last year in London. He helped make many social situations less awkward. His name is Sir Raeford Crumby. He…he assured me he has no intention of getting married. I never concern myself he will suddenly wish to become betrothed to me. He is an amusing companion and a perfect foil in large groups of people where I should otherwise be forced to mingle with eligible men."

"You astound me, Sophia!" Her aunt studied her intently. "All this because of a painful lesson learned when you were sixteen?"

She nodded, scowling. "I am terribly afraid to be vulnerable and hurt again. Now older and wiser, I comprehend people of our class rarely agree to a union that includes deep emotion or love. Perhaps I am a hopeless romantic. I could never marry without my heart being involved."

"How did you go about discouraging the men?"

Sophia chuckled. "There was one gentleman who had a great interest in the moon and the stars. He invited me to accompany him and some other avid night-sky gazers, to Hyde Park in order to observe falling stars. I declined, telling him my eyes were terribly sensitive to any type of harsh light."

Her aunt gasped. "Sophia! I can't believe you made such an absurd comment."

"On another occasion, at a ball, I had a particularly confident, aspiring suitor who snatched the dance card from my hand and scribbled his name down for a waltz. Just before the dance began, I went to the ladies' retiring room and ripped a piece of lace off the side of my gown. I gripped the loose material in between my fingers, holding it up against the skirt of my gown when I returned to the ballroom. As the gentleman walked toward me to claim his dance, I managed to bump into someone else, letting the lace fall to the floor. I claimed the collision had caused the damage, promptly excusing myself to repair it. I never returned to the dance floor that evening."

"No one in society ever guessed you are not who

you appear to be?" her aunt prodded.

She gripped the upholstered arms of her chair before replying, "Not until recently. Sir Edward comprehends the situation."

"Indeed?" her aunt exclaimed. "How did that happen?"

"I attended a summer party at his house in the country last year. His sister Camille is a great friend of mine. We attended finishing school together. I managed to convince Sir Raeford to attend the party for companionship and support and took on the role of a silly, frivolous girl that all my female acquaintances are quite familiar with. A shallow woman concerned with nothing other than her complexion, her wardrobe, and her hair. I played a memorable game of billiards with Sir Edward, and his friends Lord Millington and Lady Emma at the party. They tolerated my presence, treating me exactly as I hoped, a foolish lady with no thought for anyone other than herself."

"How did Sir Edward discover your deception?"

Sophia frowned. "I did not comprehend the identity of the man we came upon injured in the middle of the road, until I brushed the hair off his face, and he opened his eyes to stare up at me inside the carriage. Concern for Sir Edward's well-being and the extent of his injuries made me momentarily forget to pretend. Too late, I remembered to don my guise. He had glimpsed my true self. He promptly called me out for my deceit."

Chapter Six

"Be careful with my leg, man!" Sir Edward grimaced as the footman assigned to assist him with his morning ablutions tugged on the blanket wedged underneath his injured limb.

"I am sorry, sir." The young man dropped the bedclothes as if they were hot irons. "The coverings are bunched up. I tried to straighten them."

He sighed deeply, vowing never to ride a horse in bad weather again. "Leave it for now. Reach in the side pouch of my bag. Bring me my tooth powder and brush. Then find a basin for water that won't be too awkward to balance on my lap."

"Yes, sir." He bent over the leather satchel to rummage through the pockets.

A smattering of footsteps and the sound of several hushed voices reached Edward's ears. He struggled to push himself up against the tousled pillows as the noise became louder and closer. He recognized something familiar about the tone and quality of speech he heard. "Who…?"

"Edward? Are you here? Oh, my poor boy! You must be more careful! I cannot bear to think of the grave tragedy we would have suffered if no one found you!"

"Mother?" He stared at his parent as she walked into the room, clasping her handkerchief to her chest with shaking fingers. She reached up to pat the corners of her eyes with the scrap of material. "How…how did you know…?"

"Sophia wrote to us, you ninny!" With that inelegant pronouncement, his sister Camille strode into the chamber closely followed by a tall, smiling gentleman with thick corn-colored hair brushed back off his high forehead. "Lord Surd happened to be taking tea with us when Mama received the note. He insisted on escorting us to your sickbed."

He managed a stiff nod to that gentleman. "Lord Surd, please excuse my manners. I can't manage more at present. I am told I won't be able to get out of bed or move my leg for several more days."

"Sorry to hear that, Sir Edward." The gentleman replied, bowing at the waist. "It cannot be easy for someone as athletic as you to be confined to the sickroom."

He grunted his agreement. "I am as weak as a lamb."

"Here is your tooth powder and brush, sir." The footman stood at the back of the crowd of visitors surrounding the bed.

"Oh, yes, I'd forgotten." He reached out to clutch the items. "See about the basin, will you?"

"Yes, sir!" He bowed and left the room.

Lady Collins stared after the retreating man. "Never tell me that person is Mr. Canning's valet? You are the sole heir to a large property. Isn't he very young for such important responsibilities?"

Edward couldn't stop himself from chuckling, albeit tiredly. "You do not understand, Mother. Mr. Canning is in London. I trust his valet is with him. Mrs.

Canning offered the lad to assist me until I am able to send for Hawkes."

Camille laughed as she reached out to put a hand on his shoulder. "You hit your head hard, Brother. You cannot believe, once your whereabouts were known, your devoted valet would simply cool his heels at Horsham House until you sent for him?"

"Well, yes, I did." He scowled as a wave of pain suddenly reverberated up his leg. He put his head back against the pillows, closing his eyes, taking several deep breaths. "Forgive me…"

The sound of someone loudly clearing their throat echoed inside the bedchamber. "Lord Surd, Lady Collins and Miss Collins, please, I must ask you to leave the room."

Edward opened his eyes wide, looking frantically around the room as he struggled to sit up. "Hawkes? Is that you?"

"Yes, sir, I am here." His unfailingly, dependable valet reached behind him to smooth the tousled pillows before gently lowering him back against them. "You will feel more like yourself in no time."

"Ha!" Camille released his arm, grinning down at him before turning toward the door. "I know when my presence is decidedly *de trop*. Come on, Mother, Lord Surd, we must allow Hawkes to work his magic on my brother. We can visit again later when he is feeling more the thing."

"Get some sleep, my dear," advised his mother as she followed his sister.

"I will keep them entertained. Do not be concerned," Lord Surd promised before following the others.

Edward let out a gusty exhale, closing his eyes once more as the door shut behind his visitors. "I warn you, Hawkes, I am as feeble as a kitten. The dirt and grime from the road that attached itself to me when I fell off Seymour presently covers most of my body. I'm to keep my injured leg as still as possible. I desperately need a shave, but I doubt I can sit up for long periods of time. A bedpan is tucked underneath the bed for my use. How do we remedy this untenable situation?"

"You lie there and rest, sir, while I obtain hot water and clean towels and sheets," Hawkes grunted. "I will contrive. The most important thing is to concentrate on getting your strength back."

"I don't know what I'd do without you," Edward mumbled before he drifted off to sleep.

A few hours later he felt much better. His valet had managed to give him a creditable shave and a rudimentary bath using wet cloths. His rumpled, dirty shirt and torn breeches were replaced with a freshly ironed linen nightshirt. With the help of the coachman John, the groom Peter and a couple of footmen to keep him as still as possible, they raised him off the bed, using several sheets pulled taunt underneath his prone body. While suspended in this manner, Hawkes removed the soiled sheets, replacing them with fresh linens.

"Is there anything else I can get you, sir?" Hawkes bent over to gather the dirty sheets and towels strewn across the floor.

"I am exceedingly famished," he moaned. "The surgeon informed me earlier today I must partake of only gruel and a small amount of bread, in order to avoid stomach pain from eating too much too quickly."

Hawkes frowned as he clasped the pile of linen against his chest. "I will speak to Cook. Surely a small amount of beef or chicken broth is not harmful, something to hold you over until the evening meal."

"Thank you. Even broth sounds delicious," he assured his man with a grin. "I trust it will help curtail the constant growling noises coming from my stomach."

A knock sounded upon the door. "May I come in?"

He rolled his eyes in exasperation as he heard his sister's voice. "Yes."

Camille stepped inside the room almost bumping into Hawkes. "Oh, I am sorry. I didn't see you there."

"Good evening, Miss Collins." His valet managed a bow to his sister from behind the mountain of sheets and towels before he turned back to Edward. "I will return shortly, sir."

Camille strolled over to stand by the bed, studying him in an intent manner. "You are looking much better. I brought someone to cheer you up. Come in, Sophia."

She walked slowly into the room, looking lovely in a round gown of soft lavender matching her eyes. Silk ribbons of slightly darker shade were threaded through the edge of her sleeves and along the top of the bodice. "Hello. I promise you, I never suggested this."

He studied her woebegone expression. "Did my sister force you to visit me?"

"I do not understand!" exclaimed Camille. "I thought you were the one who saved Edward from perishing in the middle of nowhere with a broken leg, Sophia?"

She frowned at him before replying, "Yes, I did."

Camille turned to contemplate him. "Surely there is

reason to be grateful to her?"

He took a deep breath. "Yes, there is."

"Then why are you acting like a cross patch when you speak to her?" Camille enquired.

"Do you realize…?" He stopped speaking when he saw the look of consternation on Sophia's face.

"Do I realize what?" prompted his sister, tapping the toe of her slipper on the wooden floor.

"Stop that infernal noise." He winced. "You are giving me a headache."

"Changing the subject, huh?" Camille turned away, frowning at Sophia. "I have just recalled you were reluctant to visit my brother when I made the suggestion. At our finishing school, you were accustomed to being the center of attention. Is it disconcerting for someone other than yourself to be receiving our primary regard?"

"I required more care at school than the rest of you," Sophia pointed out, in a demure manner as she stared at the floor, her creamy complexion flushed.

His sister shrugged her shoulders. "I daresay you didn't comprehend how your behavior appeared to us. I remember often being out of patience with you. You were continually bemoaning something. It was imperative you obtained silk ribbons in a special color for the sleeves of your favorite gown, or you complained of the harsh sunlight bringing an unsightly blemish to the tip of your nose when we took a stroll in the park."

"Enough!" He vowed to question Sophia at a later time about the school, but he comprehended his sister would keep going over and over the subject like a dog chewing on a bone. "This is all remarkably captivating, but I wish to speak regarding Lady Sophia's present less than favorable opinion of me. I have not been my usual charming self over the past few days and cast no blame on her for not wishing to see me."

Camille gave him an angry look. "Very well, I understand both of you are skirting the issue and will drop the matter at present. We have strayed from the original purpose of our visit. We are here to offer encouragement. Isn't that correct, Sophia?"

She made her way inside the room coming to a halt at the foot of his bed. "I sincerely hope your brother receives news of our plans with some sign of happiness."

He glared at both women. "What are you two up to?"

Camille reached out to smooth his rumpled blanket. "I thought you might wish for company this evening. We obtained Mrs. Canning's consent to set up a table in here so we may all join you for the evening meal."

He frowned at them. "I appreciate your attempts at improving my spirits, but I cannot imagine a more terrible plan. The surgeon has decreed I am not allowed to eat anything more than soup or gruel and a bit of bread. Do you expect me to lie here and watch all of you put abundant, delicious morsels of food in your mouths without complaint?"

His sister grinned. "You will be ecstatic to hear Mrs. Canning just informed us the surgeon stopped by the kitchen before he left to amend his instructions. He told Cook you may eat a bit of stewed meat, soft vegetables and mashed potatoes tonight!"

He released the breath he had been holding.

"Thank goodness! The rumbling noises coming from my stomach are nearly as bothersome as the pounding in my head."

"Now that you are feeling less grumpy, I will leave Sophia to keep you company," Camille abruptly announced. "I promised Frederick er...Lord Surd I would take a stroll in the garden with him."

"But..." Sophia stopped mid-sentence, as Camille ignored her, striding out of the room.

"Are you afraid to be alone with me?" He couldn't help taunting her.

"Afraid?" She made a snorting sound through her nose. "In your present predicament, you are as dangerous to me as a newborn baby!"

He chuckled. "Ha! I am not referring to my prowess now, rather to my previous insistence on knowing why you are playing this game. Tell me, I gather your apparent selfishness at the school played a part in the ruse?"

"No! I...I have nothing more to say on the subject." She crossed her arms across her chest, glaring at him. "I repeat what I said earlier. You hit your head harder than you thought. Do not include me in any of your pranks. I can make no sense of what you are referring to."

He grunted, nudging his chin against the high collar of his night shirt, as he contemplated a possible reason for her contrivance. "Very well, you may evade the issue for now. I will discover the truth for myself."

She gave a brittle-sounding laugh. "You speak as though we will be spending much time alone together."

"I am tied to this bed for several days," he clarified. "I understood your visit here at Canning

House is for the foreseeable future. It is to be expected I will see you on occasion."

"Not at all," she retorted. "There are many things I need to attend to while I am here. Now your fever has broken, I made no plans to visit your sickroom."

"Ha! You confess to being the one who caressed my fevered brow!" He chuckled, vastly entertained by her admission.

She pursed her lips together and glared at him. "You tricked me, you knave! Of all the back-handed, sneaky things to do!"

"Are you vexed with me?" He smirked, gloating in the knowledge of having the upper hand at the moment. "I previously informed you that your schemes didn't hold water with me. I comprehend all your tricks and circumventions."

"Not all of them, Sir Edward!" she exclaimed in a triumphant manner before turning away, striding out the door.

Chapter Seven

He placed her in a quandary. Sophia frowned at the image staring back at her in the mirror. Josephine brushed out the long, thick strands of her raven black hair before braiding it into a dense coil, fastening it with a comb at the crown of her head. Sir Edward's questions were becoming more frequent and much more direct. Her plans had endured without predicaments for so long. It was quite easy to discourage gentlemen actively looking for a biddable wife by becoming a shrew and very simple to act the self-centered girl at finishing school. If her father ever learned of her deceptions and disowned her, the success of her face lotion insured she had enough money to set up her own household. Sophia chided herself for coming to her aunt's home without deliberating seriously on the role she should play while staying with her. She had presumed there was no need to worry about potential suitors here in the relatively quiet countryside. The uproar caused by Sir Edward's injury when she first arrived, caused her to become less vigilant about her assumed guise. Now she paid a high price for her carelessness.

What should her role be at dinner tonight and all subsequent time spent in Sir Edward's company? Thoughts, notions, and ideas whirled around in her head as she pondered the problem. One consideration and certainly the most prudent, she must continue to play the parts serving her immediate needs. Hopefully Sir Edward held his tongue. He stopped himself earlier just before he spoke to Camille about her deception. Perhaps she could secure an opportunity this evening to promise to answer his queries at a convenient time if he agreed to keep quiet about her assumed guise for the duration of his stay. Aunt Joan obviously held concerns about the role she had decided to adopt, but she appeared sympathetic to her reasons. Sophia trusted her not to say anything to the others. Sir Edward's mother, Lady Collins, expected her to be unlikeable and selfish. She severely tried that lady's patience at the house party last summer, after asking Sir Raeford to join her there without an invitation. Camille would have no reason to question her aspect because her selfish traits were quite like those she had adopted in school. There was no reason to expect Lord Surd to spend much time with her, other than at dinner when everyone else's attendance served as a foil to discourage detailed questioning from him. There was little chance her silence would be remarked upon if she made certain to keep her discourse at meals to a minimum.

Her maid signaled she had finished with her hair. After a final glance at her reflection, Sophia stood up from her dressing table, taking the shawl Josephine held out to her. A knock suddenly sounded upon the door. "Come in."

The door slowly opened. Aunt Joan stood on the threshold with her hand upon the doorknob. "Hello, my dear. Are you ready? I thought we could go down to dinner together."

"Good evening." Sophia walked across the room,

to kiss her aunt's cheek. "I want to make certain you understand how terribly sorry I am for the upheaval in your household caused by Camille's suggestion."

Aunt Joan looked confused by her comment. "Oh, are you referring to her scheme of serving meals in Sir Edward's bedchamber? It is no bother, I assure you. It is a simple matter of moving a table and chairs into the room. Because his chamber is located on the first floor, the distance to the kitchen is actually closer than the dining room."

"I am very relieved to hear that." She turned to Josephine. "I will see you later."

Her aunt stepped into the hallway. "It certainly proved to be a good suggestion. Sir Edward's situation, confined to his bed for several more days, is less than ideal. The country hours we adhere to on our estate mean the meal will be served early in the evening. We must find other ways to break up the monotony."

"Yes. Yes, of course," Sophia agreed, closing the chamber door behind her, before wrapping the shawl across her shoulders. "I must apologize again for Camille. She can be rather headstrong when she gets a notion in her head."

Aunt Joan put a hand on her arm, speaking softly. "Before we go downstairs, I must inquire, do you intend to continue to play the role you previously adopted?"

She scowled before replying in a whisper, "I must. I backed myself into a corner. With only Sir Edward to deal with, I could simply deny any dissimilation to him. However, now with Camille, Lady Collins, and Lord Surd present, I need to continue my act for their benefit. If I abandoned the pretense now, the news of my deception would quickly become common knowledge in London."

"Is such a thing possible?" Aunt Joan asked with a frown. "Camille is your long-standing friend. Her mother and Lord Surd are more than mere acquaintances. Couldn't they be trusted to keep your secret?"

Sophia sighed. "I learned long ago society's thirst for gossip or anything out of the ordinary is unquenchable. I am also aware Lord Surd resides in London for a good part of the year. I understand his valet has joined him here. The most trusted servants comprehend more about our private lives then we can ever imagine. The deception would be generally discussed in the metropolis within a fortnight, upon Lord Surd's return there. I would become an instant target as a wife for those gentlemen wishing to banish any thought in society's minds that I had hoodwinked them. And that is exactly the situation I am trying to avoid."

Her aunt paused, taking a moment to reply. "As you know, I grew up in Scotland, never spending much time in London. Are titled men in the metropolis so crass and unfeeling to force you to wed them to save face? Do they not care for affection in their marriage?"

"Love is rarely involved. The entire business of acquiring a wife is seldom looked upon with any tender emotion. It is a task, a duty if you will, to be ratified by middle age in order to insure the succession. The undertaking may contain a silver lining, if the lady in question comes with a large dowry. This is used to refill the family coffers, often substantially drained because of excessive gambling, drinking, and costly mistresses in the years before the gentlemen are ready to settle down."

"Hmmm." Her aunt studied her before speaking. "You make the whole process sound very discouraging and unromantic. I wish…I wish you could meet a man who would love you for who you are. Duty pales in comparison to that wonderful emotion. It pains me to know you will never experience such a lovely state."

"Please do not worry about me, Aunt." She forced a smile to her lips, clasping the other lady's hand in her own before leading the way down the stairs. "I am quite content as I am. Your own experience brings me great pleasure. You were able to marry a man who cares for you with a strong, lasting affection. Unfortunately, true love is an emotion most of us never get a chance to know."

"There you are!" Camille's strident voice rang out as they reached the bottom of the staircase. "I wanted to inquire, Mrs. Canning, if you wished for us to meet in the drawing room first, or should we gather in my brother's chamber?"

The butler Hendrik strode into the enclosure at that moment, clearing his throat before saying, "Madam, excuse me, Sir Edward is asking to speak to Lady Sophia. He wishes to do so before the rest of the dinner party gathers in his room."

Aunt Joan looked at her with brows raised. "Sophia?"

"Yes, I will go, Aunt." She stood up straight and tall with her chin jutted out, to give herself a sense of confidence before turning away to stride down the hallway.

"We will be having drinks in the drawing room,"

her aunt called after her.

"Whatever can my brother need to discuss with Sophia?" she heard Camille comment as she put her hand on the chamber door and knocked.

"Come in."

She twisted the knob and opened the door, poking her head into the room. "You wished to speak with me?"

Sir Edward glared at her from his perch against the pillows. "Yes, I did. Are the others nearby?"

"They are in the drawing room having drinks."

"Come in. Leave the door open," he advised her, curtly. "I suppose I must take a chance on the servants overhearing our conversation."

"They are occupied with the dinner preparations," she clarified, taking a few steps inside the room to stand beside the table and chairs.

He studied her for a moment, clearing his throat before speaking softly. "There is not much time. Let us be honest with each other. Because of your continued refusal to be frank with me by admitting you adopted a role instead of being your true self, I am forced to play along with your deception. Will you at least admit to your game?"

She clasped her hands tightly in front of her as she gave him a direct, unflinching glare. "Yes. Yes, I will. I promise to explain more later. Please do not mention anything to the others."

He grunted. "I imagine your reputation would suffer greatly if word of your hoax reached London."

"My father would be very angry with me as well," she pointed out, in a subdued tone.

He raised his brows, his green orbs flashing. "You

also deluded your parents?"

She refused to be constrained by the brows or by the umbrage reflected in his eyes. "Of course. There have been many moments of exasperation as well as confusion brought on by my mannerisms. They have become accustomed to my caprices and rarely question them any longer."

"You are in the devil of a pickle!" he exclaimed, lifting both his arms up toward the ceiling.

"No! Never!" Her denials came quickly but words failed her when his movements caused the nightshirt to bunch at the waist, exposing the side of one muscled thigh to her admiring regard.

"What, has the cat got your tongue?" He studied her briefly before glancing down at himself. "Oh! I apologize. This blasted nightshirt!"

"Please do not be sorry on my account."

He stopped shoving the material down over his limb and looked at her. "I want to make certain you understand, with your assistance, I will come around this predicament! Thank you for agreeing to play along."

He laughed, ignoring his rumpled garment. "You are welcome!"

"Excuse me." Aunt Joan stepped inside the room. "I wanted to inquire if I should delay dinner?"

"No need, Aunt." She smiled reassuringly at her before turning back to Sir Edward. "Are we finished with our discussion?"

"Yes, we are done for the present," he murmured, as he hastily pulled the blanket up to cover himself. "Please bring on the food, Mrs. Canning!"

She studied them both before answering, "Very

well, I will let Cook know."

Sophia moved to follow her from the room, pausing with her hand on the doorknob to whisper, "By the way, my aunt is in on the deception as well."

He scowled at her. "Good of you to inform me."

She grinned at him. "If you will excuse me, I am off to procure a glass of sherry."

"A capital notion," he replied, chuckling. "Bring me a bit of brandy as well."

She frowned. "Isn't that against surgeon's orders?"

"Take pity on me! Call it a boon for my agreement to play along with your game."

"You certainly make a point there!"

"Dinner is ready to be served!" Aunt Joan strode in the room, followed by the butler holding a tray containing two glasses, one half full and the other containing a splash of golden liquid. Behind them came Lady Collins, Camille, and Lord Surd. "I asked Hendrik to bring the drinks."

Sophia picked up a goblet as the butler bowed to her, proffering the tray. "Thank you."

"Before you remark on the diminutive quantity of liquid in your glass, Edward," spoke out Lady Collins. "With the laudanum you are taking for pain, an excessive amount of spirits is not recommended. The surgeon advised a splash of brandy before dinner and a small quantity of wine with your meal."

He grunted as he held the brandy glass up in front of his face. "I didn't plan to comment on it, Mother. I am grateful for anything resembling daily life before my injury occurred, even if it is only a taste of spirits."

Camille giggled. "Very well spoken, Brother. I wager you will be cross as an angry bear with a bee buzzing in his ear at the end of a week, lying here in bed with nothing to do."

"Sit down, everyone," her aunt ordered. "I will take the place here at the end. Lady Collins, you may sit on my right side, Camille on my left. Lord Surd, next to her, and Sophia, you take the seat next to Lady Collins."

A large fire burned in the fireplace. Sophia removed her shawl, folding it in half, before placing it on top of a nearby cabinet. She took her chair at the table. Several footmen entered the room carrying plates, cutlery, and an empty wooden tray. This was placed next to Sir Edward on the bed.

"You are going to be miserable," Lord Surd agreed to Camille's earlier observation about her brother, before picking up a serviette and dropping it across his lap. "Do you play chess? I could join you in a game."

"Perhaps Mr. Canning has some books on the history of the area in his library you could borrow?" suggested Lady Collins. "It couldn't hurt to gain additional knowledge about this region to compare with your own properties."

"Good of you to remind me of my neglected duties at Horsham House, Mother. I do play chess, Lord Surd. Thank you for the offer."

The footmen returned, placing bowls of soup in front of each of them while Hendrik poured wine in their goblets. Sophia picked up her spoon, stirring the rich, brown broth around bits of carrots, onion, and potatoes. She sniffed the steam appreciatively. "The soup smells delightful, Aunt."

"I'm going to take my time and enjoy every bite," clarified Sir Edward, as the butler placed a bowl of strained liquid on his tray. "Perhaps I will fool myself into believing I consumed more food than I actually did."

A few minutes later, the soup bowls removed, her aunt spoke out. "I would like to make a suggestion. I want to clarify that the feasibility of my idea must be determined by the surgeon before anything could be done. Do any of you recall my husband's infamous duel with Lord Castlereagh a few years ago?"

"Yes, of course I do, Mrs. Canning," Lord Surd answered quickly. "I thought it a very unfortunate occurrence."

"Yes, well, we did our best to hush up the whole affair," the lady replied with a blush. "Not many comprehended how close Mr. Canning came to being seriously injured. The bullet hit him in the thigh very near to the main artery in his leg, a few more inches and the loss of such a large quantity of blood could easily have been fatal to him."

"Oh, no! How terrible, Aunt!" Sophia clutched the edge of the table with one hand. "I did not realize how grievous the impairment was."

"As I mentioned, we did our best to keep most of the details secret." She paused to allow a servant to place a plate of sliced beef, mashed potatoes, and cooked squash in front of her. "While the wound healed, it took several days before my husband could place any weight on his limb. We asked a local carpenter to fashion a wooden chair with wheels. It is fitted with a kind of sliding shelf that allowed his injured leg to be elevated. The chair gave him freedom of movement between the downstairs rooms, during the period he could not walk. It is stored in the attics. I thought it would be something you could use, Sir Edward."

"What a capital notion!" exclaimed Camille, cutting a piece of beef before she stabbed it with her fork. "What do you think, Brother?"

He slowly lowered his spoon to his bowl, a semblance of a grin appearing. "It is brilliant. I must admit I couldn't imagine simply lying here in bed, inside this room, for so many days on end. Thank you so much, Mrs. Canning!"

She nodded her head at him in a regal manner. "You are very welcome. But as I mentioned, the surgeon must approve its use first."

"I cannot imagine any other outcome than his agreement," commented Lady Collins. "It sounds the perfect solution, a way for Edward to obtain a change of scene each day, while at the same time keeping his leg immobile so he may heal correctly."

"I hesitate to put a damper on your hopes, but we should be realistic," Lord Surd pointed out. "This requires lifting him in and out of the chair, and then back into the bed. His physician may feel the extra movement will be a risk to proper recovery."

"Agreed." Sir Edward frowned. "I certainly do not want to be required to walk with a cane for the rest of my life, simply because I refused to keep still and rest."

"How easy is the chair to maneuver?" Sophia asked as she experienced a disconcerting thought. She did not want him to discover her activities inside the garden shed. "Did my uncle go outdoors with the contraption?"

Sir Edward arched one of his black brows and stared at her. "What is outside that you do not want me to see, my lady?"

"Why…Why, what a devious mind you have, Sir Edward! I simply wish to understand how easily you would be able to get around without assistance," she countered blithely, biting her lip in frustration when she blushed.

"Ha! Your cheeks are turning pink!" He pointed a finger at her. "Tell me that is not a sign of guilt!"

"To answer your question, Sophia," her aunt paused to clear her throat. "As long as the surface is flat and relatively smooth, the chair can be moved easily by the occupant. However, I advise assistance at first. The wheels are rudimentary in fashion, requiring an understanding of their operation initially, but they serve their purpose well."

"Excuse me, Sophia and Edward, could one of you explain what occurred to make you both despise each other?" Camille asked, before taking a sip of her sherry. "The situation makes me excessively uncomfortable."

No one addressed her query. Thankfully, hunger won out over inquisitiveness. The only sound for several minutes was the clanking of various pieces of cutlery against the plates, as morsels of food were speared, spooned and eaten.

A knock suddenly sounded upon the chamber door. It opened and Hendrik strode inside.

"I am sorry to disturb you, madam." The butler nervously poked a shaking finger inside his shirt collar. "Lady Sophia's maid wishes to speak to her mistress immediately. I gather it is a matter of some importance."

Sophia stood up from her chair, dropping her serviette onto the table. "Excuse me. I will go see what is wrong."

She walked out of the room to encounter Josephine standing at the end of the hallway, gripping her hands together. "My lady, I have something awful to tell you. The shipment of face lotion has been destroyed!"

She put a finger to her lips, turning around to make certain the chamber door was closed, and Hendrik had returned to his post in the entry. "We cannot talk here. Come with me to my room."

She swiftly ascended the stairs with her maid following close behind. They slipped inside her bedchamber. She closed and locked the door behind her. "Now, you may speak."

"Oh, my lady!" Josephine wailed. "I was afraid this might happen!"

"I am losing patience," she warned, crossing her arms across her chest, glaring at her.

"I am…I am sorry, my lady." Her maid wiped at the tears coursing down her cheeks with the back of her hand. "John asked the coachman to tie your crate down securely. He did as he requested and told him not to worry. It occupied a proper place wedged between two others."

"Yes?" she prompted, impatiently.

"Well, a stray cat ran in front of the mail coach just as it left." Josephine paused to take a shaky breath. "The horses reared. The crate fell off and crashed to the ground."

"Did John recover it?" she asked, with a frown.

"Yes, he did, my lady. He brought it back. It is inside the shed," her maid confirmed.

"There is no time to lose. Several of my most important customers in London are waiting to receive their orders." She pulled her watch out of a pocket concealed in the folds of her gown. Nearly seven o'clock. "We must check the crate immediately to determine the extent of the damage. I hope not all of the bottles were destroyed."

"What…what will you tell the others, my lady?"

She stared at the floor pondering the predicament. "I will instruct Hendrik to inform them I received an urgent note from my mother asking about a recipe for a special remedy to reduce lung inflammation. One of her dear friends just happens to be suffering greatly from the malady."

"Lud, my lady!" her maid exclaimed. "You are good at comin' up with those stories!"

"Regardless, I need to make haste. You stay here. Both of us cannot go traipsing about outside. If I see Cook, I will tell her I need to obtain some oranges from the tree in the kitchen garden to send to my mother. I heard they are often prescribed to fight inflammation."

Chapter Eight

Edward watched the servants remove the table and chairs from his room. When they finished, Mr. Gordon entered to check his leg. He took advantage of his presence to question him about using the wooden chair. The surgeon told him bluntly it was too soon to be thinking about getting out of the bed. Of utmost importance, was to concentrate on keeping his foot as still as possible. Without offering any additional words of advice, Mr. Gordon abruptly turned away and walked out of the room. After such a glum, unenthusiastic reaction from the surgeon to his inquiry, Edward resigned himself to an early night. He ordered his valet to help him wash and don a clean nightshirt before leaning back against the pillows with weary groan, a book clasped in his hand. With nothing much to occupy himself with in the coming days, it was a perfect time to ponder on the quandary he continued to be preoccupied with. *What happened to Lady Sophia to cause her to go to such great lengths to avoid marriage?*

"Do you require anything else before I leave, my lord?" Hawkes questioned, standing near the door.

"No. Stop." He struggled to sit up as he caught sight of a folded shawl on top of the cabinet. He pointed to it. "Give me the wrap. Tell Lady Sophia's maid to request her mistress to come visit me before she retires for the night."

"Does it belong to the lady, my lord? I can deliver it to her servant."

He cocked an eyebrow at his valet, frowning at him. "What? You want to go and spoil my ruse, Hawkes? No, certainly not. Do as I ask."

The man picked up the garment, holding it out to him, sighing before answering, "Very well, my lord. Good night."

"Good evening," Edward called after him, tucking the wrap behind his pillow.

Edward waited for Lady Sophia to arrive. There was no doubt she would eventually make an appearance. He thought about the various deceptions she practiced and attempted to comprehend the reason she resorted to such complex artifice. If a woman did not choose to wed, surely she could simply make that fact known and accepted by any prospective suitors? Even as the conjecture crossed his mind, he acknowledged as a daughter of a titled lord, her wish to remain single would never be countenanced in society. Getting married, running a large household, bearing children, was as natural as losing teeth and growing new ones for a woman of her status.

What made her fight the normal order of things? Why did she go to such great lengths, even hiding her true personality to eschew matrimony? He considered the many verbal exchanges they exchanged since arriving at her aunt's home. While she often answered with light-hearted banter in response to his goading comments, he sensed a brittleness, a fragile sensitivity behind the teasing comebacks she made to him.

"Ah ha!" The reason suddenly dawned upon him, like a lightning bolt flashing across the night sky. Someone severely bruised her feelings. It was almost certainly a matter of the heart. The event probably occurred when she was a young, impressionable girl. She still suffered. The emotional wound festered deep inside of her. To protect herself from additional pain, she chose to abstain from all possible sentimental, romantic ties with men. That was almost certainly the answer!

"Why must you insist I come in person to retrieve my shawl? Your valet could easily have given it to my maid." She stood on the threshold glaring at him, her glorious violet-hued eyes glowing like the most brilliant amethyst.

"Who hurt you?" he asked the question bluntly without equivocation, intent on observing her reaction.

She gasped. "I…I…what did you say?" She reached out to grip the doorknob, holding on to it with whitened knuckles.

"Come over here." He dropped the book he still held onto the blanket before stretching his arm out straight, curling his fingers at her. "I cannot discuss this with you standing on the other side of the room. Leave the door ajar."

She shut her eyes for a moment before opening them again, her body visibly shaking. Her hand slid off the knob, causing her to stagger at the sudden loss of support. She stood still for several seconds, taking deep breathes before training her gaze directly on him. She slowly walked to the side of the bed. "I do not understand."

"You insist on playing me for a fool!" he growled

at her, as he experienced a simmering, zealous rage deep inside his chest. "I thought you agreed to be honest with me!"

She blinked at him. "I meant I cannot imagine how you guessed."

"I assumed too much too quickly. I apologize." He bit his lip, chastising himself for believing the worst, and responding with such fury. "I overreacted and am unsettled by my own actions. There is no explanation for my current turbulent emotional state. Perhaps it is compensation for the whack received on my head. But somehow, I sensed for you to go to such lengths you suffered profoundly, intensely, and concluded it was a matter of the heart. I imagine you were hurt when you were young and vulnerable."

"Oh!" She took several deep breathes through her nose before pursing her lips together and frowning at him. "Are...are you usually so perceptive?"

"No, never." He reached out to gently clasp her wrist, encircling it with his fingers. "I will attempt to explain. From the moment I opened my eyes inside your carriage and observed you staring down at me, I became conscious of a sense of empathy for you. You will disregard this perception because you believe I am frustrated and bored, lying here for hours on end in this bed and think it is merely a random notion to keep myself entertained. You would be wrong. Yes, my temper is short, I am in considerable pain and far from happy. However, there are few distractions causing me to be intensely mindful of my surroundings. For some reason, I find myself acutely aware of your inner sensibilities and emotions. Do you think you can believe or make sense of this?"

"Yes…yes, I…I understand," she replied, keeping her gaze trained on him. "I too am acting out of character. I let my guard down. I have never, ever done such a thing. It would have been best to ignore you lying on the floor of the carriage. I should not have visited this room and taken care of you when you were in the depths of fever. But I couldn't leave you to suffer alone in either situation. My own subterfuge became much less important. My thoughts and concerns were for someone else for once."

"Don't be so hard on yourself," he advised her. He moved his fingers to cradle her palm in his hand. "I believe you wore your disguise as a shield, a way to carry on, to cope with life. Am I correct?"

Her hand closed over his in a tight grip. "Yes…yes. There was no other way for me to contend with what happened."

He studied their wrapped fingers. Her nails were creamy white with blunt tipped ends. "I will not ask his name. Do you know if he is still alive?"

"He is," she replied, with a sigh. "His two elder brothers both passed away. He inherited his father's title and estate. He lives there with his wife and two children."

He frowned as he heard the listless, passive tone of her voice. She had done more than build a wall around her heart, there was a moat to vanquish as well. He adopted a nonchalant tone. "Other than the unexpected deaths of his brothers, it sounds as if his life experiences turned out well."

"I imagine it was not easy to suddenly become master of a large family estate," she replied, shrugging her shoulders. "When I spent time with him, he never thought of ever being required to assume such a large responsibility. He mainly spoke of pleasurable diversions and aimless pastimes. We...We often discussed the countries we planned to travel to."

"How did you meet?" he inquired, keeping the resonance of his voice just above a whisper.

She scowled before answering. "We were never formally introduced. His family visited friends that had recently settled on an estate near my home. I was out walking early one morning. He...He suddenly emerged from a connecting path and asked if he could join me. I...I spent the most happy, enjoyable two hours of my life with him that day. When he suggested we meet in the same place every morning during his stay, I eagerly accepted his proposal."

"How long did that go on?"

"Almost a fortnight," she paused, taking a deep breath. "He suddenly informed me that his family planned to leave on the night of the twelfth day."

He studied her with concern. "I note you say the words *suddenly* and *night*. I take it his departure was unexpected?"

"Yes. Yes." She released his hand as if a hot poker burned her skin, turning away from him to walk to the other side of the room with her arms crossed over her chest. "He...He came to my home the evening before they left. There had been a...a flood at his family's estate. His father needed to return immediately to survey the damage."

"He visited your house?" he asked with surprise. "You introduced him to your family?"

"No." She turned around to look at him, her cheeks flushed. "He never met my parents. He believed they would not understand how we felt and thought they would say we were too young to recognize deep emotions. We agreed to keep our relationship hidden."

He frowned at her, attempting to make sense of what she told him. "He met you in secret that evening? You came to an understanding?"

"No, never any kind of formal arrangement." She stared down at the floor, her hands clutched together. "He…He threw rocks onto my bedchamber window that last evening. I had pointed it out to him several days before. I opened the window to see him standing in the shrubbery below. He told me what had occurred, mentioning he and his family planned to leave early in the morning. He thanked me for the enjoyable time we spent together. I never saw him again."

"Damn!" The oath burst from his mouth before he could stop it. "Excuse my language. I now get a clearer understanding of your reasons for resorting to a grand deception. Your shattered hopes when he failed to appear the next day, the heartache you experienced after you understood he truly left, the thought of a close relationship with any other gentleman must be unimaginable."

"I…I cannot believe it!" she exclaimed, staring at him, trembling.

"What? What is wrong?"

"Your description of my feelings…" She took a deep breath, cupping her chin with a shaking hand. "I remember the night so vividly. After he left, I went downstairs to dinner. I forced myself to join in the general discussion and to eat a few morsels of food. Unable to continue for long with the pretense, I eventually excused myself, pleading a headache and lay awake the entire night not believing what had occurred. By dawn, I convinced myself I had imagined the entire episode. I finally fell asleep just before daylight, thinking to meet him later in the morning on my walk."

"When were you able to face the truth?"

She paused to clear her throat. "A few weeks later, I read a notice of his marriage in the paper. The life I imagined unfolding over the years disappeared in that moment."

"I can readily conceive your state of mind," he assured her. "You stood on the edge of a cliff eager to spread your wings and fly. Suddenly, the dirt loosens, cascading far below. You become unbalanced, set to topple over at any second. You eventually come to realize you must face each new day carrying that shaky foundation and mourn the loss while attemping to fashion another destiny. You continually remind yourself to be grateful for what you have and never wish for more. In time, this gives you the strength to carry on. I intend to help you carry on, to become comfortable in your own skin once more."

She smiled at him, her violet eyes glossy and bright. "Thank you for putting the intense emotional journey I have lived over the years into words. I can now make sense of my responses to the embarrassment and pain I experienced."

"You are welcome." He frowned. "There is something I am confused about. Why were you standing alone in front of the Covington mansion the other evening?"

She blushed, looking down at the floor. "It was a misunderstanding. I was waiting for my mother to join me. Our carriage arrived soon after I spoke to you to take us back home."

The chamber door suddenly opened wide to reveal his sister. She studied them with raised brows before speaking. "You are here, Sophia? I hope you two settled your differences."

"It helps to discuss the issues," she admitted, giving him a warm smile with trembling lips.

"We came to an accord. What is it you require, Sister?"

Camille frowned at him. "You continue to be mum on the subject. Very well, I hope one of you will explain your conundrum to me at a later time. I wished to inform you, Brother, Lord Surd needs to return to London. He agreed to escort us to Horsham House on his way to the city. Now that Mother and I have assured ourselves you will survive and recover, we believe it is best to return. We leave you to concentrate on getting stronger and back on your own two feet once again."

"Very thoughtful of you both. You plan to depart in the morning?"

"Yes. We will come to say good-bye before we leave. Don't sulk too much, Edward. I hope you can convince Mrs. Canning and Sophia to continue to share their meals in here with you. It is not a good idea to spend your entire day lying on the bed staring at the walls. You will suggest doing so to your aunt, Sophia?"

"Yes, I will," she agreed in a soft, meek tone of voice, avoiding his gaze. "My aunt mentioned serving meals in this room was an easy task since it is situated on the main floor near the kitchen."

"The chairs and table will need to be moved in and out," he clarified. "I hate to be the cause of such upheaval."

"Camille?" his mother called out, as she stepped inside the room. "There you are. Finish saying good night, please. Your brother needs his rest. We leave early tomorrow as well. I trust your sister has already informed you of our plans, Edward?"

"Yes, she has." He grimaced as a sudden twitch of pain coursed through his leg. He lay back against the pillows with a ragged sigh. "I…I will say good-bye in the morning."

"As soon as you are better and able to travel home, I will invite Miss Cather to come stay for a while," his mother informed him.

He sat up again with a start. "Why ask her to visit?"

She stared at him with brows raised. "I am certain Camille would welcome her friend's companionship. Miss Cather can keep you company as well. It will be some time before you are able to resume your various duties on the estate."

"May I take my shawl?" Lady Sophia stepped forward.

His mother started at the sound of her voice, turning around. "Oh, I did not see you there. I trust you will find some time away from your own concerns to keep my son entertained while he is confined to this room?"

"Mother!" he exclaimed as he reached for the wrap tucked behind his pillow.

"Please do not fret!" Lady Sophia murmured to him, as she strode up to the bed, gripping the shawl in one hand. "I plan to do my best to find time, Lady Collins."

"Your answer is more than I expected," his mother

acknowledged. "I appreciate that."

"All is settled then," his sister announced before hurrying across the room, putting a hand on her mother's arm and the other on Lady Sophia's, guiding them both toward the door. "Good night, Brother."

"See you in the morning," he muttered as his arms gave way beneath him, and he collapsed flat on the bed. He frowned up at the ceiling, studying the wavering images cast there by the last bit of light from the candle before it burned itself completely out. It would not be a simple matter, the obligation he had resolved to accomplish. He mentally pushed away the nagging question of why he bothered to attempt such a thing. He avoided acknowledging the real reason, choosing instead to pick an obvious one. There was plenty of free time to make certain his vow ended in success.

Chapter Nine

After filling most of the remaining jars with leftover face lotion and repacking another crate, Sophia tiredly crawled into her bed. She tossed and turned for most of the night, finally falling into an exhausted slumber just as the sun rose. She woke much later when bright daylight pierced the curtains on the window near her bed. She sat up, yawning as the chamber door slowly opened.

"My lady, are you well?" Her maid tiptoed into the room, grasping a tray in her hands.

"Yes, I am fine." She pushed back the blanket, swinging her feet to the floor. "I experienced a difficult time falling to sleep last night."

"You worried me, my lady." Josephine put the tray on the table near the fireplace. "It is not like you to stay in bed so late. I brought you a pot of tea, an egg, toast, and some of Cook's marmalade."

"I will try to eat. I am not very hungry." She yawned again and then put on her slippers before picking up the shawl she tossed on the back of a chair the evening before. "I packed another crate last night. Please take it to John. It needs to be on today's mail coach. There is also an order for more bottles on top. I do not have many left. Make certain that gets taken as well."

"Certainly, my lady." Her maid bent over to stir the

glowing coals in the hearth before walking across the room to pick up the parcel. "I will be back in a few minutes to help you dress."

"Very well." Sophia wrapped the shawl across her shoulders and sat in a chair in front of the plates of food and the tea pot. She went through the familiar motions, pouring some tea into a cup, adding milk and sugar before taking a sip of the hot beverage. She closed her eyes, sighing as the warm liquid slid down her throat.

A knock suddenly sounded upon the chamber door.

She quickly opened her eyes, sitting up straight in the chair. "Yes?"

"It is me, Sophia. May I come in?"

As her aunt's voice reverberated through the door, her stomach flipped and flopped underneath her rib cage. It was not a sign of hunger, she acknowledged to herself as she put a hand over her belly. Last night's personal revelations to Sir Edward caused her to experience a severe amount of emotional upheaval. She hesitated to open more of those long-buried wounds with her Aunt Joan's observant, searching queries. However, as a guest in her aunt's home, she must be amicable as possible with her in return for her gracious hospitality. She took a deep breath before calling out, "Yes…yes, you may."

The door opened. Aunt Joan walked into the room, a somber expression on her face. She shut the door behind her and walked across the room to settle in a nearby chair. "How are you? We missed you at breakfast. Camille expressed her regrets not to be able to say good-bye. Sir Edward is also concerned over your continued absence."

"They left already, then?" she questioned,

deliberately avoiding making any comment about Sir Edward's feelings.

Her aunt turned toward the fireplace mantel, appearing to study the face of the ornate clock that decorated its top. Fortuitously, the timepiece chimed nine beats before she spoke. "Morning is well advanced, Sophia."

She sighed, placing her cup back on the tray, pulling the ends of her wrap across her shoulders. "Yes, it is."

"Is there something bothering you, my dear? It is not like you to hide away in your room. It might help to talk about whatever is upsetting you."

She reminded herself of the discussion earlier with Aunt Joan about her own experience meeting and falling in love with Uncle George. Perhaps she was the best person to confide to about her present, befuddled state. Hopefully, she could shed some clarification on her dilemma. She had told her most of the story anyway. "I would appreciate your opinion."

"I promise to give you the best advice I can," her aunt replied, reaching out to lightly squeeze her arm before taking a seat across from her.

"Thank you." She paused as she pondered the best way to begin, deciding it would be prudent to tell all and not leave anything to chance. "I…I received a summons of sorts last night, from Sir Edward's valet, to visit his master to retrieve the shawl I left behind after dinner. Needless to say, I was exasperated by his presumption. Such a menial task could easily be performed by my maid! I didn't hesitate to make him aware of my displeasure when I strode into his room a few minutes later. He brought me to a standstill with one question."

"What did he say to you?"

"He asked, '*Who hurt you?*'" She let out a shaky breath. "In that moment, all the painful feelings and misery I kept buried inside for almost five years, came to the surface. I knew I couldn't hide anymore. I understood it was imperative to acknowledge what happened."

"Did you tell him everything?"

"That is what is most surprising," she answered, frowning at the glowing coals in the fireplace. "I did not need to describe what occurred. He already guessed most of it."

Her aunt gasped. "My goodness! Very few people are able to decipher other's life experiences. I would never have believed he could be such a perceptive individual."

"Nor I. He expressed surprise as well and speculates it is due to his heightened powers of observation while confined to his bed. The most astonishing thing proved to be his description of my sensations after Da...my friend left. He comprehended I had talked myself into believing I misunderstood my friend. I thought to see him again the next morning ready to go on a walk together. Sir Edward also mentioned the heartache I certainly suffered when I finally understood I would never see Da...my friend again."

"Well!" Aunt Joan sat back against the cushion on the chair, frowning at her. "It is no wonder you experienced trouble sleeping last night. The hurtful memories were once again brought to the surface. I can imagine it was difficult for you to calm yourself and relax."

"You do understand!" She came to her feet, striding across the floor to stare out the window. "Since the discussion with Sir Edward, I feel as if a deep wound I thought healed has reopened once more."

"I am very sorry to hear that, Sophia. I trusted, with the passing of so many years, in your ability to calmly look back on the experience as an example of emotional mistakes we all make when we are young."

She whipped around to face her aunt. "I wish I had the sense to feel that way. I understand now, as long as I kept up the pretense, giving potential suitors a disgust of me, there was no need to face the truth of what happened. Last night's discussion forced me to relive the final time I saw the one man I believed I could ever love. My heart feels as if it is being squeezed tight by the boning in my corset. I can barely breathe. It is a terrible sensation!"

Her aunt studied her for several seconds before she spoke. "Perhaps it is a good thing this happened. The reopening of a distressing, highly emotional wound will hurt in the beginning, but with the passing years you will gain wisdom and clarity about the circumstances. I am certain you will find the ability to look at what happened when you were sixteen calmly and rationally. The painful sensations will go away."

"I trust you are correct." Sophia made her way across the room to sit down once more. "Until now, I avoided acknowledging the experience and the lessons I learned from it."

"You must accept the mistakes you both made before you can move on." Aunt Joan stood up, patting the top of her head with her hand. "Do not expect the weight of your pain to lift overnight, my dear. I will leave you to finish your meal."

After she left the room, Sophia forced herself to eat a couple bites of toast and most of her egg. She pushed the plate away and had sipped the last drop of tea when Josephine returned.

"All finished, my lady?" Her maid reached out to stack the plates on the tray.

"Yes, thank you." She put her empty cup back in the saucer and stood up. "Will you lay out my yellow walking gown? I need to get some fresh air."

"Of course, my lady."

Sophia strolled over to her dressing table, sitting down on the chair in front of it. The surface of the table was cluttered with some cotton cloths she used to wrap the bottles the evening before. She reached for one of the larger discarded pieces, intending to fold the material for use in a later shipment. As she gripped the edge of the cloth, a full bottle of face lotion tipped over, rolling across the flat surface of the dresser. "What is this? Oh, no!"

"My lady, what is wrong?" Her maid rushed across the room to stand at her side.

Sophia picked up a scrap of paper and read the neatly penned name across it. She staggered to her feet, toppling the chair over backward onto the floor. "I missed this last night! It is for Lady Anne Mackey. Of all my customers she is the most loyal. You remember, Lady Mackey was the first one to try my solution and subsequently champion its healing qualities. Mr. Hoover informed me she required more lotion just before we left the city."

"What can we do, my lady?" Josephine bent over

to pick up the overturned chair.

"Quickly now, I need to dress and take this to town. Get me my brown walking gown." She took off the shawl, throwing it onto her bed and grabbed her pocket watch from the nearby table. "It is nearly ten o'clock. The vial must be on the mail coach to London today."

"Yes, my lady." Her maid ran across the room to the clothes press, yanking the door open.

"Do you know how far away the posting house is? Could we walk there?" she asked as she leaned over the washstand in the dressing room, splashing cool water on her face.

"We could, my lady, but we'd never make it in time." Josephine dropped the gown she requested onto the bed. "It must be over two miles."

"We need the carriage then," she replied without further consideration. "I will finish dressing. Go inform John to ready the vehicle and drive it in front of the house."

"My…my lady, they already left…left with the crate you gave me earlier."

"Oh, no!" she exclaimed, putting her palm to her forehead in frustration. "Never mind the gown. I need my riding habit. Go to the stables. Tell them to saddle a horse for me. No old, plodding mare, mind you!"

"You are going to go to town without a chaperon, my lady? How can I leave when you're not dressed? You will never fasten them buttons!"

"Do not concern yourself with such trivial matters as buttons. I can do some things on my own!" she informed her with exasperation, as she placed the label with the lady's name and address on the bottle "I will return before anyone knows I left and will take a footman or groom with me. Tell Hendrik I require someone to escort me. Make sure he understands his mistress is not to know of my plans. This bottle must reach London as soon as possible. You may come back here after you give my orders."

As soon as the door closed behind Josephine, Sophia quickly unbuttoned her nightgown, hurriedly stepping out of it, leaving the garment in a crumpled heap on the carpet. She reached for her shift, dragging it over her head, pulling it down across her breasts and hips. She tied the drawstring closed at the back of her neck and reached for her short stays that laced in the front. She pulled the skirt on her riding outfit up to her waist, tucking in the ends of her shift before shoving her arms into the long sleeves on the matching spencer jacket. With shaking fingers, she eventually closed all the fastenings at the front of the garment. After pulling up and tying her stockings to her garter, she wedged her feet into sturdy half-boots and then reached for her brush, dragging it through her long, waist length hair, deftly twisting it into one thick strand. She secured it on the crown of her head with a tortoise shell comb. She had just placed a hat decorated with a jaunty purple feather matching her eyes on her head when the chamber door burst open.

"You are to go to the stables when you are ready, my lady," Josephine announced breathlessly from the doorway, while she gripped her hands together. "Are you quite certain this cannot wait?"

Sophia grabbed the bottle of lotion from the dresser, placing it securely inside her reticule before tightening the strings at the opening. "I already explained why this must go to the city without delay. There are other products readily available at other chemist and apothecary shops in London. Lady Mackey could easily take her business elsewhere. She tried mine first and continues to champion my mixture. This is a matter of pride and self-respect for me. I cannot treat someone who has been a loyal follower so shabbily."

Her maid pulled a handkerchief out of her pocket and blew her nose. "Very well, my lady."

Sophia strode across the room toward the open door. "See that those unused cloths are folded and put away before my aunt spies them and asks questions."

"Yes, my lady."

Sophia hurriedly made her way down the stairs and across the hallway to the corridor leading to the kitchen.

"There you are! We missed you at breakfast this morning."

She came to a sudden halt, muttering words that should not be part of her vocabulary as she heard Sir Edward's strident voice addressing her, forgetting she needed to pass his bedchamber on the way to the back door. Sophia peered inside the room to find him sitting up against the pillows grinning at her.

"Good morning! I promise to be at the table for the evening meal. I...I will see you later."

"Where are you going in such a rush?" he bellowed, frowning.

She sighed with frustration before answering, "There is something very important I must take care of."

"More secrets, huh?" he grunted.

"I have no time to discuss the matter with you," she informed him, in a manner brooking no argument as she stepped back into the hallway. "Good-bye."

She made her way to the back kitchen door without encountering any additional interference and strode through the garden to the trail leading to the buildings behind the house, soon reaching the stables. She spotted a brown mare with a white star on her forehead and a side-saddle on her back. A groom stood next to the horse, holding the reins. A large black horse also saddled and ready for riding, ambled nearby, nibbling on a patch of grass.

The man bowed to her. "My lady, this here is Betsy. She is a fine, steady horse. I will accompany you."

"Very good." She stepped up onto the mounting block. "What is your name?"

"It be William, my lady." He led the mare over to her side.

"Thank you, William." She turned around with her back to the horse before sitting in the saddle and taking the reins in her hands. She secured the ends of her reticule around the pommel on the saddle, allowing it to dangle over the side. "You understand we need to make our way to the posting house with all possible speed? I must ensure an important package is on the mail coach to London."

"Yes, my lady. The coach stops next to the Red Lion on High Street," the groom answered as he sat atop the other horse. "I know the quickest way to get there."

"Excellent! Lead on!"

They cantered swiftly across the fields soon making their way to the center of town. As William led them down High Street, Sophia looked over his shoulder and noticed her coach with Peter holding the horses' heads, pulled over to one side of the road.

"Stop here," she called out. "Peter, where is John? Has the mail coach left yet?"

Peter turned his head at the sound of her voice, looking at her with a startled expression on his face. "My lady! Yes, the crate is secured to the coach. It is over yonder."

"Thank goodness it hasn't gone!" she exclaimed as she studied the various vehicles parked near the spot he indicated. Other than the mail coach, carrying several trunks and crates tied to its roof as well as an overweight matron with a floppy hat and a cleric clutching a torn, tattered bag, both hanging out of each of the windows, there were also several dashing, brightly colored curricles drawn up nearby. "I have something else needing to go to the city. Where is John?"

Her groom hesitated before he spoke, slowly raising one finger to point. "My lady, he be inside the…the pub having a pint."

She turned to study the building he indicated. "Is the mail coach driver inside as well?"

"I…I believe he is, my lady," Peter replied.

"William, follow behind and help me dismount," she told him. "You can hold the horses' heads."

"You never mean to go in there, my lady?" William asked with an arrested expression on his face.

"No, my lady!" Peter shouted.

She frowned at each of the men before flicking the reins, guiding the mare forward. "Both of your reactions are entirely uncalled for! I am required to complete a very important task. It will be done! Make way for me, William."

She gave him no choice but to lead her horse across the street. He dismounted first before silently turning to offer her his arm. As she grasped his wrist with her hand and carefully lowered herself to the ground, she heard a loud ruckus coming from inside the pub. Several voices were raised in hearty laughter and jeers. She heard the distorted voice of a man call out, '*Time for a quick tumble before we leave for London?*'

"Are you certain, my lady?" William frowned at the building.

She hesitated a moment before reminding herself of the importance of her errand. She squared her shoulders, standing up straight in a confident manner before turning away to unfasten the strings on her reticle, lowering it from the saddle with shaking hands. "Yes, I am. Wait for me here. I will return shortly."

She walked inside the open door to the pub, to be momentarily blinded by the darkness inside after being out in the bright sunlight. There was a sudden lull in the boisterous conversations. A niggling sense of fear, combined with a jittery nervousness caused her heart to beat loudly in her ears and her palms become sweaty inside her gloves. "John. John, where are you?"

"Over here, my lady," his voice rang out from a place on her left.

She turned toward the spot to see the blurred outline of her coachman in the wavering candlelight.

"Look what I found!" Hot breath, smelling of fried onions and spirits fanned her cheek as a man bent over to block her progress forward. "The lady is ripe for plucking!"

"No!" She stepped away from the stranger, while

frantically pulling at the strings of her reticule. She felt the bag open, and she wedged her hand inside, to clutch the bottle of lotion. She pulled it out, waving her arm over her head. "John, take this. It needs to go inside the crate to London."

The container left her hand. "Yes, my lady. You'd best leave now."

"Sophia?"

She gasped in shocked surprise. Her heart clenched at the sound of the cherished voice she thought to never hear again. She turned toward the dimly lit interior of the pub, observing the silhouette of a dark-haired man with a rumpled, untied cravat hanging loosely across his chest, sitting at a nearby table. A serving girl sat draped across his lap making giggling noises, while alternately licking his earlobe. He shoved the woman away, staggering to his feet.

"Da…David?"

She studied the man's face. In those moments, she quickly became conscious of feelings of extreme dread. The bits of toast she nibbled on earlier crowded into her throat, threatening to gag her. Dear Lord! It could not be him! He lurched to one side as he attempted a fixed stance in front of her. Even in the dreary light from the candles, she experienced an all-consuming horror and she gulped as bile surged into her mouth, forcing the sour liquid back down to her stomach. David's face appeared bloated, and his eyes were no longer the shiny, deep blue color she remembered. He looked at her as if from behind a heavy mist. The awareness of repugnance increased as she chastised herself for wasting so many years languishing over a shadow of a man. She couldn't hide the absolute sadness and despair she knew in that moment. She turned away, stepping over loose boards on the rough wooden floor to reach the door. "I…I must go."

"Sophia, no! Let me explain." He followed her outside putting his hand on her arm, clutching the sleeve on her jacket. "In my youth, my mother made a pact with a dear friend decreeing her daughter and I were to marry each other. I could not formally agree to anything more lasting with you until I secured my release from the agreement. I intended to see to the matter without delay but shortly after I returned home, the lady's parents both died in a carriage accident. With no one else to turn to, I…I consented to marry her."

She pulled away from him, wrinkling her nose at the stale, sour stench of his breath. Without speaking, she strode down the front steps to stand on the mounting block next to her horse. Only then did she face him, forcing out fierce, bitter words from deep down inside her belly, "Did you ever give a thought to *me and my feelings*?"

Chapter Ten

"Confound this broken leg!" Edward exclaimed, smacking the sheets on the bed with his palms in frustration.

Hawkes came running inside the room. "What is wrong, sir?"

"Everything!" he yelled. "That woman is up to something. I need to discover what it is before she brings more suffering down upon her head and gives me additional problems to resolve. But I cannot move!"

"Sir! If you are referring to Lady Sophia, I am quite certain she is perfectly able to take care of herself. Now lie back and rest."

"Tell me the minute she returns," he sighed in resignation as he reclined backwards against the pillows. He looked toward the open door as he heard someone clearing their throat.

"Sir Edward." Hendrik bowed from the entry. "There are visitors to see you. Shall I tell them you are not receiving?"

"Visitors! Who is it?"

The butler coughed into his fingers before replying, "Lord and Lady Millington, sir."

Before Edward could react, a gloved hand grasped Hendrik's shoulder, moving him aside out of the doorway.

"What did you do to yourself, old man?"

He frowned at Lucas, standing on the threshold grinning at him. "I will thank you to keep your amusement to yourself. I warn you, I am in a black mood and in no fit state for anyone's company even if you are my good friend."

"Sir?" Hendrik still hovered nearby.

"You may leave. You go as well, Hawkes. This will not take long," he informed them before turning back to Lucas. "How did you know where to find me?"

"Emma and I left home for London to visit her sister and family," his friend apprised him, while pulling off his gloves. "On the way, we decided to stop by Horsham House to return your previous call to us. Imagine our surprise when we overtook Lady Collins and your sister on the road several miles south of here. They told us what happened and where you were staying."

He grunted. "You interrupted your trip to come gloat at me, is that it?"

Lucas drew his brows together and scowled at him. "Do you believe I am so heartless?"

He took a deep breath, releasing the air through his mouth. "I cautioned you. I am sorry. I am devilishly blue gilled. I wish I could get out of this blasted bed."

His friend pulled a chair away from the wall to sit nearby. "I can imagine feeling equally frustrated and angry in your position. Will you tell me what happened?"

"I will relate what I can remember," he paused, gazing at the closed door. "Where is your wife? Did you not say she is here with you?"

Lucas grinned at him. "Emma is chatting with Mrs. Canning. I thought it better to determine the true extent of your injuries before she joined us."

"Exceedingly wise of you. Did you note the name Canning?"

"Yes, but I had no opportunity to inquire of the lady's extended family," his friend paused with an arrested expression on his face. "Is there any connection to the illustrious George Canning?"

"She is his wife," he chuckled, enjoying the incredulous stare Lucas gave him. "I count myself fortunate to be taken in by such illustrious company here in the wilds of Berkshire."

"She came upon you?" prodded his friend.

"No…no, I am indebted to someone else," he hesitated as the sound of hurrying footsteps reverberated from the hallway.

"Here they are!" announced Mrs. Canning, as she strode inside with Lucas' wife following behind her. "I received a summons to attend my niece in her bedchamber. I will leave Lady Millington in your care, my lord."

"I will gladly take on the responsibility." Lucas grinned as he stood up and reached out to clutch his wife's hand. "Come say hello to the patient."

"Is anything the matter, Mrs. Canning?" Edward sat up, grimacing as he blurted out his query.

"I am certain it's nothing of great concern," she replied, reassuringly. "She most probably wants my advice on a gown to wear to dinner tonight. I will see all of you later."

Emma led her husband across the room until they were both standing at the side of the bed. "I hope you do not mind we accepted Mrs. Canning's invitation to stay overnight and enjoy a meal with you this evening,

Edward?"

"No, no! It will be good to have your company," he assured her as he lay back once more.

She studied him for a moment before turning to Lucas. "Has Edward told you who rescued him and brought him to South Hill Park?"

"We were just touching on the subject when you walked in," he answered her with lifted brows. "Care to elaborate, my dear?"

She grinned up at him before replying, "It turns out Lady Sophia Hampton is Mrs. Canning's niece. She was traveling here for a visit when she came upon Edward lying unconscious, with his leg twisted underneath him, lying in the middle of the muddy road."

Lucas turned to him with an expression of surprise on his face, "A circumstance shockingly convenient for you, old man!"

"I do not see anything agreeable about what occurred," Edward retorted peevishly.

"I am not suggesting your injury is a good thing," his friend clarified. "But surely you can acknowledge it is to your benefit you are being cared for in an illustrious government official's home as well as having a familiar acquaintance to converse with while you are laid up in this manner?"

"Well yes, I certainly agree with the first of those sentiments. But I regret to inform you, there has rarely been a chance to speak to Lady Sophia."

"Of course not!" Emma giggled. "Did you forget her first concern in life is herself?"

"No! You…" Edward shut his mouth, biting on his lip. It was wrong to come to Lady Sophia's defense when they were oblivious to her deception. What a pickle!

"Out with it, Edward," Lucas ordered. "I can't imagine you were going to tell us she is no longer the annoyingly selfish lady we all dealt with at your home last summer?"

"Perhaps my injury forced her to think of someone else for a change," he explained, choosing to follow the middle ground with his answer. "Her attitude is much more tolerable when I do see her."

Emma studied him without speaking for a moment. "Indeed? I look forward to observing this wondrous transformation for myself this evening."

"As do I," Lucas added with a grin. "I suppose miracles can happen."

Emma reached out to touch his shoulder. "Did you clear up the mystery of what occurred at the Covington mansion?"

He frowned. "I haven't been privy to the entire story. She alluded to a misunderstanding."

Hendrik appeared in the doorway and bowed. "Excuse me, Lord and Lady Millington, the housekeeper informed me your room is ready. Would you please follow me?"

"Come, my dear, let us remove the travel dust from our clothes." Lucas took Emma's hand and placed it on his sleeve as he guided her toward the open door. "We will see you later, Edward."

"Very well," he mumbled his reply, deliberating on the change in circumstances. How was he to handle this new, awkward situation?

"Is my patient better today?"

He turned his head, frowning at Mr. Gordon as he

appeared in the doorway. "When may I get out of this confounded bed?"

"Precisely the reason I am here," the man answered jovially as he walked inside the room, placing his bag on the chair, and making his way to the foot of the bed. "I checked the construction of the push chair Mrs. Canning has offered for your use. If you promise to keep your leg as still as possible for one more day, I will agree to allow you to use the chair for a brief airing outside the day after tomorrow. Are you happy?"

He grunted. "It will be a great improvement on my current situation."

The surgeon pursed his lips together, crossing his arms over his chest, glaring at him. "I thought to hear a more enthusiastic response from you."

"Can you imagine being forced to rely on others for your most basic needs?" he muttered, drawing his brows together, glaring at him. "Do you comprehend how humiliating it is? Not only do I dream of being able to walk without help, but it is also my greatest aspiration to take care of myself once more."

"I am sorry, sir." Mr. Gordon strolled to the side of the bed. "I realize it is extremely trying for you to lie here helpless day after day. But it is the only way to make certain the bone heals in a proper manner."

He sighed. "I understand your reasoning. I am very eager to go on the promised excursion."

"That is better. I gave your valet instructions on the operation of the chair. If I am not needed urgently elsewhere, I will be here to supervise your removal from the bed in the late morning the day after tomorrow."

"Thank you."

"You are very welcome, sir. You need to be patient. You will be on your own two feet walking normally before too many weeks go by."

He took a deep breath as Mr. Gordon left the room. How could he keep a serene countenance in the days ahead? To be forced to be inactive in this manner would surely drive him mad.

"Are…Are they gone?"

He looked up at the sound of Lady Sophia's voice, and observed her standing on the threshold clutching the nearby wall. "At last you visit me! I inquired as to your whereabouts for most of the morning."

"You…you didn't answer my question." She kept the tone of her voice barely above a whisper. "Lord and Lady Millington…where are they?"

"They went to their room. Your aunt invited them to stay the night. You will see…" He suddenly noticed her creamy complexion was completely altered from its normal, healthy color. Her skin appeared ashen-gray, and she swallowed convulsively as if she were about to cast up her accounts. "What happened? Come over here and tell me."

She slowly let go of her grip on the wall, wavering as she well-nigh lost her balance. She frowned down at the floor, perhaps making a silent plea for strength. Creeping and plodding, her feet shuffled forward. With awkward steps, she dragged herself toward him before bumping against the chair Lucas had used earlier. Her knees buckled at the contact, and she plopped down onto the seat with a grunt. "I'm sorry…sorry. I…I came to tell you I…I will not be present at dinner tonight."

"What the devil?!" He sat up in the bed, ignoring the sheet as it fell away from his chest. "You're alarming me! Inform me at once what occurred to affect you so. You are a pale, weak shadow of your former self."

"I…I am not surprised you will not allow me to retreat without…without an explanation." Her lips trembled for a moment as she made an attempt to smile but the effort appeared too great. She winced instead. He heard her take a deep breath before murmuring, "I…I saw…saw him this morning. In town."

"You…" he stared at her afflicted countenance, gasping in shock as the meaning of her cryptic statement hit him like a fierce, direct punch to his stomach. "You…You encountered the man who hurt you?"

"Yes." She reached down with a shaking hand to clutch the fabric of her gown as if it were a lifeline, as she swayed from side to side on the chair while staring ahead blankly, her lovely violet-hued eyes devoid of any spirit or sparkle.

He did not speak as he intently observed her countenance. The change in her arresting as if a flame on a candle had suddenly been extinguished. "Tell me what occurred. Why were you in town?"

She stayed silent as she stared down at her hands before looking up at him with a trace of some vibrancy in her eyes. "I…I suppose what happened today is not truly important. It is the realization of wasted devotion I gave to him for so many years that hurts the most."

He registered the fact she had avoided answering his query and resolved not to press the issue. "You still care?"

"When you say the word *care,* if you are referring to an emotion that still has the power to give pain, the answer is a resounding *yes*. If you asked me that same question yesterday, my answer would have been emphatically *no*." She turned away from him so he could not see her face, but not before he spied a tear rolling down one cheek.

Nothing prepared him for the deep-seated ache, like a heavy clamp across his chest, that consumed him when she started crying. The pain was acute, momentarily robbing him of air. He closed his eyes, willing himself to remain calm, to breathe deeply. Gradually he experienced a perception of composure. He exhaled and opened his eyes to discover her direct gaze on him. Traces of tears were still apparent on her cheeks, but she had collected herself.

He dislodged the press of emotions, forcing out what he sensed would be the most significant observations he had ever given, in his lifetime, "I...I wish to ask you something, Lady Sophia. I...I want to explain the reason for my query first. Most of us, male and female, form some type of emotional attachment to others when we are young and impressionable. Because of our innocence when we experience the attraction, we tend to believe it an all-consuming, everlasting emotion. Very rarely is that belief the correct one. We recover from the temporary state of enchantment quickly and continue on with our lives, carrying a wealth of knowledge and understanding to better serve us as we grow older and wiser. My question to you is this: why does your experience appear to be different? Why have you decided to carry the weight of a passing, youthful attraction to such an extent that you devote the rest of your life to ensuring any gentleman who considers making you his wife will quickly banish the thought from his mind?"

She came to her feet, clutching the back of the chair for support, clearing her throat before speaking. "It is expected gentlemen and titled peers of our class marry equally matched, exalted women. You called me *lady*. It is my rightful title, but you are wrong to describe me so. I am not a maiden. I am not chaste or unblemished. Forgive me. I…I must go."

Chapter Eleven

"Here is the tray, my lady." Her maid placed it on the table in front of her.

"Thank you. You may go." She forced the words from deep inside her throat, staring blankly at the glowing bits of coal in the fireplace. She requested her aunt visit her earlier. A fierce pounding in her temples caused her to rescind the appeal a short time later.

"Please, my lady, you must eat something," Josephine fretted.

She frowned at the interruption and turned to look at her. "I will make the attempt. I cannot promise more. Please leave."

"Very well, my lady, I will return shortly." Her maid sniffed into her handkerchief before she bustled to the door.

"Stay." Sophia took a deep breath. "Tell me, are the others beginning the meal downstairs?"

"No, my lady, I believe they are having drinks in the drawing room."

"I will join them." She spoke quickly, not wanting to question her decision. "Go inform Hendrik, tell him not to say anything to my aunt and then come back here to assist me."

"Yes, my lady." Her maid rushed out the door, closing it softly behind her.

She stood up and walked across the room to her

dressing table. She sat down on the chair, staring at her reflection in the mirror. For almost five years she resolved to forget David, to acknowledge she would never marry and raise a family. For her parents' sake, she continued to attend parties and balls while surreptitiously discouraging any possible suitors. After suddenly being confronted by the weak, cowardly representation of the man she once thought to spend the rest of her life with, why should she retreat and hide after all she had done to adapt and survive in the world?

The door opened again, and Josephine strode inside. "I gave the butler your message. Which gown will you wear, my lady?"

She pondered her choices and came to a decision. "The black crepe gown with jet beads trimming the bodice and the long sleeves. I am especially fond of the embroidered crepe roses on the bottom of the skirt."

"Very good, my lady," her maid answered, as she rushed over to the clothes press.

A few minutes later, Sophia wiggled her feet into black chamois leather shoes before sitting down at her dressing table once again. "Part my hair in the center. Braid it into a crown on my head. There isn't time to do more."

"Yes, my lady." Her maid reached for the brush, separating the thick strands into three parts. She quickly braided the long tresses and secured it.

"Thank you. That will do. Please fasten the clasp on this for me." She stood up, reaching for her matching black jet necklace, handing it to her maid.

"There we are. All finished, my lady."

Sophia studied her refection in the full-length mirror. Other than slightly flushed cheeks, she appeared much as usual. "Thank you. You managed in record time. I will see you later."

"Enjoy the dinner, my lady." Josephine curtseyed to her before turning away to gather up discarded articles of clothing on the floor.

She reached for her favorite lavender colored silk shawl, taking a deep breath as she draped it across her shoulders and strode out of the room into the hallway. She hastened across the landing to descend the stairs, not wishing to cause unnecessary delay of the serving of the evening meal.

She rounded the corner at the bottom of the stairs and nearly stumbled into Lord Millington, standing just outside Sir Edward's bedchamber.

"Oh, I apologize, my lord." She clutched the nearby wall for support.

"Lady Sophia!" He turned to her with brows raised. "I understood you were not joining us for dinner."

"Sophia?" her aunt's voice rang out from inside the room.

"Yes. I am here." She walked inside as Lord Millington stepped back with a bow, to allow her to enter first. "I am feeling much better."

"I am so happy to hear that, my dear!" Aunt Joan beamed at her. "I believe you are acquainted with Lady Millington?"

She curtseyed to her. "It is lovely to see you again, my lady. Congratulations on your recent marriage."

"Thank you." Lady Millington studied her. "We were together at Sir Edward's house party last summer. You managed a grand entrance there as well."

"Good of you to join us, no matter how it was accomplished," commented Sir Edward as he favored her with a piercing glare.

"Sit down, Sophia," Aunt Joan urged. "How very convenient! Hendrik already set a place for you!"

"My maid informed him I planned to join you for dinner." A footman pulled out a chair for her and she sat down.

Lord Millington settled himself across the table, next to his wife. "I understand you are the one we should thank for coming to Sir Edward's assistance."

Her cheeks warmed as she glanced over at the patient to find him grinning at her, obviously enjoying her discomposure. "I assure you I did nothing out of the ordinary, my lord. Only a callous, insensitive person would continue on their journey, leaving someone lying injured in the middle of the road."

"If you listened to your most respectable, proper maid, you would have left me there," Sir Edward pointed out.

"A fortunate circumstance for you, her appeals did not sway me," she countered, frowning at him.

"Tell us, how did you manage the rescue?" asked Lady Millington.

"My coachman and groom fashioned a make-shift cot and were able to lift him onto the floor of my carriage," she informed her.

"Never say they moved him with his leg broken!" Lord Millington exclaimed.

"Not at all, my lord," she quickly assured him. "My coachman previously served as a batman during the war with much experience setting broken bones. After finishing that task, he collected two stout limbs to hold Sir Edward's injury rigid and secured it with rolls of cloth I carried inside my bag."

"He expressed his gratitude to you once safely stowed inside your carriage?" Lord Millington inquired, with a grin at his friend.

"Ha! There was no opportunity. Initially, I proved insensible. Lady Sophia had no notion," Sir Edward clarified.

"Indeed? When did you discover who you rescued?" Lord Millington questioned her with an intent look.

She cleared her throat before answering. "He…he opened his eyes, and I comprehended his identity."

"Admirable!" Lady Millington dropped her serviette on her lap and picked up a spoon. "Sir Edward's brilliant green eyes certainly are unique."

"Providentially, Lady Sophia's destination happened to be close to where my accident occurred," Sir Edward pointed out. "I am very thankful to her and her aunt, Mrs. Canning for allowing me to stay here and for putting up with my provoking fits and starts while I recover."

"You are very welcome, Sir Edward," her aunt acknowledged. "I am glad I could be of assistance."

"I must warn you, Mrs. Canning," Lord Millington spoke out in a grave manner, "knowing his character as well as I do, Sir Edward will be worse than a caged tiger in a few days after lying here in bed inactive."

"I believe I hit upon a partial solution," she apprised him, with a smile. "My husband ordered a push chair to be crafted for his use when he became injured in the leg and unable to walk for a time. With the surgeon's approval, Sir Edward plans to use it."

"Mr. Gordon stopped by to check on my progress this afternoon," he informed them. "He promised I may try the chair out the day after tomorrow."

"Such good news!" exclaimed Aunt Joan.

"In the nick of time," Lord Millington commented with a smile, as he bent over his bowl of soup.

"I am definitely looking forward to a change of scenery," admitted Sir Edward, before carefully spooning some broth into his mouth. "Lying here day after day with nothing to look at but four walls and an enticing, slightly obstructed view from the window of the garden, I am very eager for fresh air."

"There is no one to keep you company during the day?" Lady Millington inquired, with a frown. "It was a good notion to instruct the servants to serve dinner here."

"Camille's idea," Sir Edward clarified. "On occasion, I do encounter visitors. Mrs. Canning, as well as her son Charles, stopped by several times to check on my well-being."

"What about you, Lady Sophia?" questioned Lady Millington, looking across the table at her. "Oh, I am sorry. I forgot you prefer the companionship of Sir Raeford Crumbly. I trust he is taking a sojourn here with you?"

Sophia resisted an unladylike urge to squirm in her chair as the lady's words caused her to recall her callous action last summer, when she invited her friend to the house party without Lady Collin's knowledge. She cleared her throat before answering. "I attended Sir Edward in the beginning when he fought a harsh fever. No, Sir Raeford is not in residence. He is in Paris with some friends."

"You helped take care…?" Lady Millington abruptly stopped speaking to stare at her. "Forgive me.

I find the image of you coming to the assistance of others hard to imagine."

"My dear," Lord Millington murmured and placed his hand over his wife's.

"I completely understand Lady Millington's sense of disbelief," Sophia spoke out. "My behavior when we were together last year was contemptible. I...I am doing my best to make amends."

Thankfully, two servants entered the room at that moment and the awkward conversation halted. One servant gathered the empty soup bowls. The other wielded a tray holding four plates piled high with slices of beef, chunks of potatoes covered in brown gravy, accompanied by a mound of green beans. Two slices of oranges decorated the sides of each of the plates. When they all were served, Hendrik came into the room holding a bottle of red wine in one hand and a small, covered dish in the other.

The butler walked over to Sir Edward, placing the diminutive plate in front of him. He lifted the lid. "A bit of beef, strained gravy mixed with stewed potatoes and beans, for you, sir. Fresh squeezed orange juice follows."

Sir Edward frowned at the dish before sighing. "I will do my best to savor every bite."

"You poor man!" Lady Millington commiserated. "Mrs. Canning, everything looks and smells delicious. I note the fresh oranges. Is there a neighbor nearby with a conservatory?"

"Thank you, my lady," her aunt replied, as she signaled to Hendrik to pour the wine. "No, as a matter of fact, my husband hired Sir John Soane to propose some alterations to the house as well as to design and build a conservatory. Everything was completed a few years ago. The conservatory is tucked away on the south side of the house overlooking the garden."

"What a surprise, Aunt!" Sophia exclaimed, wondering why she had never come upon the structure earlier.

"It is a special thing indeed to obtain fresh fruits year-round," commented Lord Millington.

Another servant entered the room carrying Sir Edward's juice. Hendrik finished pouring the wine in all their glasses. "Will there be anything else, Mrs. Canning?"

"No, thank you. That will be all for now," she advised the butler before turning to Lord Millington. "The conservatory proved to be a costly endeavor, but the benefits more than outweigh the expense."

"I considered building one next to the kitchen garden at our home in Bucklebury," Lord Millington replied before picking up his glass. "A toast of thanks to our hostess for graciously welcoming my wife and me into her home without prior notice, and best wishes to my good friend for a quick return to form!"

"I'll drink to that!" exclaimed the patient before he took a sip of orange juice. "Delicious!"

Sophia raised her glass. "To your good health!"

"We will be able to resume our journey to London tomorrow assured you want for nothing during your recovery here, Edward," commented Lady Millington with a smile, as she lowered her glass and picked up her knife to cut a piece of the beef.

"I agree," replied her husband, forking a bean. "I believe you were incredibly lucky Lady Sophia happened to come along that particular stretch of road. I shudder to think of the horrible circumstances if you had lain there much longer."

"You are most certainly correct," Sir Edward answered with a frown, as he spooned a bit of his stew. "Did I mention the fierce rainstorm?"

"The weather proved terrible as well?" Lady Millington asked.

"Oh, yes! It had slipped my mind," answered her aunt, with her brows raised. "A sudden squall came up just before Sophia arrived. The rain lashed against the windows in the library. I worried it might cause damage to the roof."

"You were fortunate indeed," remarked Lord Millington, looking up from his plate at Sophia. "I am surprised you started on your journey here in such a storm."

She swallowed a piece of beef before replying, "When we left Slough, the sky remained clear. It started as nothing more than a light drizzle when we had completed over half of the journey. The rain fell in torrents quite suddenly just before we came upon Sir Edward."

"There is certainly no question, Lady Sophia coming upon Edward when she did was most opportune," mused Lady Millington. "Perhaps it portends something more than simply a case of good fortune. Fate or providence could be at play."

"What, ho, my dear!" exclaimed Lord Millington. "Are you attempting to put a romantic twist on the event?"

Sophia's fork dropped from her suddenly nerveless fingers, clattering onto her plate. "No! Please!"

"Enough teasing and conjecture!" called out Sir

Edward, as he thrust his empty dish away. "I do not wish to deliberate on the whys and the wherefores. Is there any dessert, Mrs. Canning?"

"Yes, there is. I instructed Cook to prepare a syllabub using lemons from a prolific tree we have in the conservatory," answered her aunt, with a concerned look at Sophia.

She dropped her serviette onto the table and came to her feet. "I...I am sorry. I find I am not as recovered as I believed. I will say good-night."

Chapter Twelve

After Edward had eaten his meagre meal of gruel, a
piece of bread and orange juice, Hawkes assisted him
with his morning ablutions. He now wore a clean, long
nightshirt that fell below his knees. He laced his fingers
behind his head as he stared up at the ceiling, pondering
recent events. Lucas and Emma left early yesterday to
continue their journey to London. He enjoyed their
company, but dinner two nights ago had been very
awkward. He ate a solitary meal last evening. Lady
Sophia requested a tray in her room. After assuring him
her niece did not feel ill, simply not sociable, Mrs.
Canning chose to eat in her chamber as well.

The door suddenly burst open. Mr. Gordon entered
the room followed by Hawkes. Behind him came a
footman pushing a large wooden chair. Lady Sophia's
coachman and groom entered last.

"Are you ready to try this?" the surgeon inquired,
as he walked over to the bed to examine his leg.

After giving a nod to the others, Edward studied
the unusual piece of furniture. A Windsor slatted seat
and back chair frame had been fitted between four
wheels. Two larger wheels were at the front of the
contraption while two smaller ones were placed behind,
with a bar attached to the back. He noted the servant
used the bar to steer the chair forward. Two wooden
planks were secured at the front of the seat. These

protruded between the front wheels.

"I am eager to get out of this bed," he affirmed. "How do you propose to accomplish getting me from here to there?"

"Let me do some adjusting first," replied the surgeon. He walked over to stand at the front of the chair and lifted the plank on the right side, anchoring it with a piece of wood wedged underneath from a spot near the front wheel. "This allows you to keep your limb elevated. Using two bedsheets placed underneath you, the four men will lift you into the chair. I will secure your injured leg with another sheet as they carry you, making certain it is not jarred in the process."

He took a deep breath. "Your plan sounds sensible. Go ahead."

The surgeon nodded. "Hawkes, you take the sheets. Hand me one and all four of you will tuck the other two underneath the patient. I need two men on each side of the bed. I am going to make a sling like this and place it under his injured leg. When the sheets are in position, gradually lift Sir Edward from the bed, and then gently lower him onto the chair. Stop if I tell you to."

The feat was accomplished without much difficulty. Mr. Gordon kept pace with the other men as they carried him the short distance across the room. He was carefully transferred to the seat of the chair. The surgeon steadied his leg and lowered it onto the protruding plank.

"We did it!" Mr. Gordon grinned broadly.

"It is a joy to be out of that bed!" Edward proclaimed. "I take it, since the wooden brace is still on, I needn't be concerned about jarring the limb while I am in the chair?"

The surgeon frowned. "You must make certain the brace doesn't tumble off the plank, causing the bone in your leg to jolt. It could possibly break again."

He winced. "A horrible consequence to be sure. I will avoid such a thing happening at all costs. Thank you all for your assistance. Will someone wheel me outside?"

"Hawkes, please cover Sir Edward with a blanket," ordered Mr. Gordon. "There is a strong, chilly wind from the east today. Mrs. Canning suggested you go to the conservatory. John will take you there."

"Very well," agreed Edward, anxious to be anywhere but inside his bed chamber. "I assume the conservatory is easily accessible?"

"Yes, sir," John spoke up. "Mrs. Canning showed me and Peter the path just to the left of the kitchen garden. We will see you arrive there safely."

"Don't overtire yourself," the surgeon advised as he picked up his bag. "I will return shortly to help lift you back into bed."

"No need to rush back on my account," Edward called out, as John pushed him toward the door.

"You don't comprehend how weak you are," Mr. Gordon clarified. "A soft mattress will be very welcome to you in an hour's time."

"I will put clean sheets on the bed while you are away, sir," Hawkes called out.

"Fine," he answered briskly, eager for a change of scene. "Lead the way, Peter."

The three of them made their way down the hallway and past the back stairs. The door leading to the kitchen swung open just before they reached it. Lady Sophia appeared in the opening. She paused, mid-step on the threshold.

"Sir Edward! Hello!" she exclaimed, flushing rosily as she hastily tucked one hand into her skirts.

"Good day," he answered her with raised brows, as he pondered what she could be hiding from him. "As you see, I obtained permission for a temporary release from my chamber. We are headed to the conservatory. Will you join me there?"

"I…I must return to my room. I will join you as soon as possible."

"Very well," he countered somberly, stung by her less than eager response. "Continue on, Peter."

The groom lifted the front wheels while John pushed the chair forward using the back wheels as they crossed the threshold. Once outside on all four wheels once more, they passed by the edge of the kitchen garden before guiding the chair down a smooth, dirt path on the south side of the house.

He took a deep breath of the fresh, cool air. "Ah, this is wonderful!"

They stopped in front of an iron-framed door with paned glass windows in the center flanked by two stone fluted Greek Ionic columns. On either side of the door were two large windows also of paned glass, to the side, a large bay window. The top of the structure had small panes of glass bordered in iron forming a shallow pitched roof ending in a glass dome-shaped cover over the bay window.

The door slowly opened a crack. An elderly man's wizened face poked out. "Will you be coming inside? Be quick about it. Don't want the heat to escape."

The previous procedure to exit his room was followed to maneuver the chair across the threshold.

Peter quickly shut the door behind them as John steered him forward into the center of the conservatory.

He studied his surroundings. Lush green ferns spread intricate lacy leaves overhead as brown trunks covered in a thick, brown furry substance bent toward the permeating shafts of sunlight. Several flowering pink camellias grew underneath in dense shade. Small trees planted in stone pots lined the walls between the windows. He caught a glimpse of several shinning fruits dangling on the branches, lemons, plums, and possibly peaches.

"When shall we return, Sir Edward?" asked John.

"In a…" He had started to tell them to come get him in a couple of hours, but then acknowledged to himself such an extended length of time out of bed on his first day of freedom would be ill-advised. "See to me in an hour."

"Very good, sir! Come on, Peter."

The heavy glass door made a swishing sound as it closed behind them.

He continued his observation of the interior of the conservatory. He watched as the old man bent over an unusual specimen with straight, pointed leaves. "What type of plant is that?"

"This here is a pineapple plant, sir," the man informed him.

"Pineapple?" he blurted out in surprise. "I never thought to see such a rare thing actually growing. How did the Canning's obtain it?"

"A gift from Sir William Pitt to my master, sir," the man told him, with obvious pride.

"Indeed?" He recalled the statesman's great influence in Mr. Canning's life and career. He took a deep breath of warm, moist air. "I detect no evidence of fumes. I understood it was a common practice to build a fireplace at one end of a conservatory with hallow walls underneath the floor, allowing the smoke to run the length of the building and heat the interior."

"At first perforated pipes lay under the rock floor connected to a coal-fired broiler." The man stood up straight, wiping his forehead with a gloved hand. "Mr. Canning believed the gas fumes to be harmful to the plants and fruit. In 1817, he hired men to remove the stone floor, adding hot water pipes. In this way, the stove could be placed outside. Heating is now done without the damaging smoke."

The door swept open. He turned to see Lady Sophia standing on the threshold.

"Come, enter quickly before this gentleman takes offense," he called out in warning.

She stepped inside, allowing the door to swing shut tightly behind her. "Hello, Mr. Grimmer."

"You two are acquainted?" he queried, with raised brows.

"Yes, ah, I spend much of my free time in the garden. I have stumbled upon Mr. Grimmer on numerous occasions."

"I…I must see to…to my seedlings," Mr. Grimmer muttered, as he gathered his tools together placing them in a worn, leather bag. He strode across the room to grip the door handle. "See this is fully closed when you leave."

She walked away from the entrance toward the bay window, bending over to study the camellias before turning to observe the entire room. "Beautiful. My aunt and uncle are very lucky to own such a unique plant collection."

"Look down, directly in front of you," he advised. "It is a pineapple plant. Do not touch the leaves. They appear to contain sharp spines."

"My goodness!" She stared at it. "Marvelous!"

"The broad leaf tree with the odd shaped green and purple pods, I wonder what that is?" He pointed to a plant a few feet away.

She strolled past him to examine the tree. "I believe these fruits are figs."

"You are quite knowledgeable."

She turned around to face him. "I am familiar with certain species."

"I suppose you are able to recite the Latin names for the plants as well?" he teased.

"Frequently, yes I can," she replied, flushing. "Are you impressed?"

"Assuredly, quite a feat," he told her, with a grin.

"A great accomplishment for a selfish, narrow-minded lady?" She scowled at him. "Is that what you meant to say?"

He studied her sour expression for a moment before answering, "I understood we had left that description behind us. I admit such a thing would cross my mind last summer, before learning of your ruse."

She sighed. "I find it exceedingly troublesome to remember which role I should be adopting in whose company."

"You made the choice to act the self-indulgent woman," he reminded her.

"Yes, I did. My dissimilation was quite easy when no one else held knowledge of my subterfuge," she countered with a frown.

"Certainly that is a quandary we should discuss. I see a bench over there in the corner," he observed. "Would you like to sit down? I need your help with the chair."

"Very well. How do I operate it?"

"There is a bar positioned and attached to the back." He pointed over his shoulder. "Use it to push the chair forward."

She moved to stand behind him. He heard her take a deep breath and then let out a grunt before the wheels began to roll forward.

"Is the contraption too heavy for you?" he asked in concern, as the chair slowly rumbled across the stone floor.

"No, no. Once started, the momentum builds and movement becomes practically effortless," she answered.

"See that the impetus does not get beyond your ability to control," he warned her nervously, as an image of an unguided push chair came to mind, his body propelled forward onto the ground. He shuddered at the gruesome, painful thought.

"I would never act so carelessly and risk injuring you!" she exclaimed from a spot near his left ear, as she maneuvered the chair around to face the front windows.

"Forgive me, I did not mean to question your abilities," he answered with a frown, as she took a place on the bench next to him.

"I understand. The thought of suffering additional agony or discomfort because of someone else's negligent actions is unthinkable."

"It is a great comfort to know you appreciate my precarious situation." He settled himself back against the seat tucking the blanket securely across his legs. "First, allow me to say the matter you mentioned at the end of our earlier private conversation is safe with me."

She turned away from him, not before he observed a deep flush covering her cheek.

"Th…thank you," she mumbled.

He looked away from her, pretending an interest in the construction of the push chair, giving her a moment to collect herself. "On the subject of your deception, I spent much time deliberating the matter. Previously, you excused the change in mannerisms on your need to assist me in my recovery. You felt obligated to think of someone else and their requirements. Could the experience of tending to me be used as a reason or an impetus for moderation or adjustment to your attitude in the future?"

She whipped around to study him. "Are you saying I should drop the ruse entirely?"

"No, no, I would recommend a gradual change," he replied quickly. "A slow, seemingly natural improvement in your demeanor. No longer deliberate on which role to adopt when in company. Simply be your true self."

"Be myself?" She frowned. "I…I do not wish to appear full of conceit, but I believe my genuine personality could be described as convivial. I am part of a titled, wealthy family. I understand I do have a pleasing…pleasing appearance. There will be offers of marriage. How am I to stop this from happening?"

"Simply give the prospective suitors a negative reply."

She snorted. "Back to the original conundrum. How am I to explain such an answer to my family?"

He pondered her question. "Pardon me, you are not a young miss fresh out of the school room, and not the heir to a title, required to form a union and have children. Is there something wrong with telling them you have no wish to be married?"

A harsh noise emitted from her mouth, a laugh sounding more like a cough. "My father would never, ever accept that answer. But you are correct. It is past time I move away from home and set up my own establishment."

"A good idea," he agreed. "There is plenty of opportunity to consider your future and make plans. I needn't inquire if you were ever kissed. Was it done properly?"

"Ever…?" she stopped, obviously confused by the sudden change in subject. "Why speak of this? I bared my soul to you. You are aware of the heartache and the betrayal I experienced when younger."

"I did not mean for my query to cause you further pain," he clarified. "I simply acknowledged out loud the probable inexperience of your young lover. No one else has ever kissed you?"

"There was the bungled embrace with Lord Dunson, the reason I am in disgrace and sent here to stay with my aunt," she retaliated.

He sat up straight in the push chair. "Lord Dunson? I thought him engaged to be married?"

"You are correct." She frowned down at her hands, clasped together in her lap. "I trust he still is. I should explain. You recall when we spoke in front of the Covington mansion? I attended their ball that evening. It was a terrible crush. The rooms were packed with people. It was ridiculously hot and stuffy. I stepped onto the balcony for some fresh air. Lord Dunson had arranged for his betrothed to meet him there. He mistook me for her. She followed moments later and saw me in his arms."

"Ha!" He couldn't hold back a chuckle as he pictured the awkward scene. He quickly regretted his inconsiderate display of mirth. "I apologize. I am certain the situation was anything but amusing at the time."

She caught her bottom lip between her teeth, looking contrite. "Naturally the circumstance was quite unexpected and shocking, but I soon experienced relief. His betrothed understood and agreed it was a case of mistaken identity. When I left, they both appeared vastly entertained by the situation. Unfortunately, Lady Covington observed the initial embrace, misconstrued what took place and spoke of it to several of her guests. Such titillating gossip spread across the ballroom. I was deemed no better than a harlot a few minutes later. When you came upon me that night, I had just escaped the uproar inside."

"And you were sent away to Berkshire. Society's loss is our gain, I believe."

Her luscious violet-hued eyes studied him for several moments. "Th...thank you for saying such a nice thing to me."

"You are very welcome," he answered, with sincerity. "Now before I embarrass myself further by giving out more compliments, I want to return to the subject of my original statement related to kissing. I am convinced your previous experience was a paltry one."

"Dash it all! I do not care what you believe!" she exclaimed before standing up, glaring down at him. She bent over his chair, her adorable button nose a mere inch away from his face. "Enough, Sir Edward! My patience with you is at an end. I did all I could to assist your recovery. I told you details about my past no one else has knowledge of. Yet you continue to toy with my emotions in a cruel manner. A moment ago, you complimented me and now…"

He put his hands on either side of her face, covering her mouth with his own, thinking only to quiet her. He stilled as he touched the supple, velvety skin on her full lips. He experienced a split second of panic. *Oh no!*

"Ah!"

He heard her sigh against his mouth. Or perhaps he experienced the sensation of it. She swayed against him. His feelings of trepidation vanished. He became consumed by a calming sensation, as if he were floating on a gentle, rolling sea. He paired the movement of his lips across hers with this new sensibility. His thoughts came as a surprise to him, but at the same time, he was certain he had never experienced anything so luscious. Gently, gently, he nibbled the pad of her lips with his teeth and then licked the corners of her mouth with his tongue.

Her fingers grazed his chin, a hesitant yet bold action, using the leverage to press her lips more firmly against his. The taste of her consumed him. He lost the ability to consider, evaluate. But suddenly feelings of guilt surfaced. *No! He must not do this! Not to her!*

He wrenched his mouth away, regarding her through narrowed eyes as he struggled for air, his chest rising and falling in a frantic, hectic rhythm.

"Is…Is this my…my p…pun…ish…ment?" Her

words came out in labored, short bits of sound.

Her question touched a sensitive chord buried inside of him. He pictured his father berating him for not being the most intelligent student at Eton, for not immersing himself in all the aspects of the daily operations of the family estate. The deep-seated fear of not having anyone trust his abilities, of never being able to prove he was capable of being a profitable, revered landowner and respected head of his family rose up to taunt him once again. He answered curtly, unwilling to explain his actions at this moment. "If that is what you believe. I sensed you were enjoying yourself."

She blanched as the sound of his cutting words filled the space between them. She stepped away, turning without speaking, grasping the handle on the glass door to swing it wide open before striding outside, running toward the house.

Chapter Thirteen

Tears overflowed at the corner of her eyes, coursing down across her cheeks. Impatient with herself for displaying such great weakness and fragility, she muttered an oath and wiped at the moisture with the back of her hands. Unable to hide the evidence of her agitation from her aunt or anyone else inside the house, she switched paths and chose to make her way to a bench she spotted previously, on the other side of the knoll at the bottom of the hill.

Settling herself on the stone seat, she tugged her shawl more tightly across her shoulders before turning toward the brilliant illumination of the warm morning sun. Normally careful to protect her unblemished skin from the potentially harsh rays, she cast aside prudence for the moment, thinking only to dry all traces of tears from her face.

Several minutes later, she stood up and repositioned herself on the other side of the bench facing away from the sun. She listened to birds singing together in the nearby trees and the soothing sounds of mooing from contented cows in distant fields. She took a deep breath, savoring the sense of calm engulfing her spirit when only a short time before she had been consumed by...*what?*

How was she to decipher the reaction she experienced from Sir Edward's kiss? She marveled again at the intense thrill as his soft lips caressed her mouth before he made the erotic gesture with his tongue. She had ceased to think or to contemplate her actions at that moment. She remembered instead an intense craving, a desperate need for more. She recalled reaching out to touch his chin, trusting the movement would indicate her keen awareness of the pleasurable sensations, hoping the embrace would proceed indefinitely.

To her delight, he had continued his impassioned salute upon her mouth. Their tongues mingled together, moving back and forth in a stimulating, sensual dance. But suddenly he pulled away, glaring at her.

She interpreted his look as one of disgust, not surprising since she had positioned herself as no better than a squalid trollop with her frenzied, greedy response. In that moment, all the pleasure she had gleaned from the embrace vanished. A deep-seated embarrassment settled over her. She sighed, gazing without seeing, at the clumps of green grass waving gently in the soft breeze. Once again, forced to relive her belittling experience at sixteen, she acknowledged her innocence and foolishness.

Of course, she had kissed David. After the first spontaneous embrace, they began to discuss their future together. Their lips came together frequently. Gradually emotions heightened, deepened. She hastily put a hand over her mouth as she recalled an especially boisterous kiss from David. He pressed against her with such vigor, her lips had flattened against her front teeth. She endured soreness for several days. It was nothing comparable to the soft, caressing touch from Sir Edward today.

The day *it* happened, they had improvised a picnic. She exhaled again as a painful, deep-seated ache worked its way up from her stomach to lodge like a brick in her chest as the memories resurfaced. She remembered she smuggled bread and cheese from the larder. David brought a bottle of ale he managed to secure without notice the day before. They spread her shawl and his coat on the grass bordering the lake and shared the feast. She laughed at a story he told her of a time he got stuck on an upper branch of an elm tree at eight years old. Suddenly she found herself pinned beneath him on the hard ground, her lips once more flattened against her teeth by his over-zealous kiss. She became aware of his hand as it traveled upward from her ankle to her hip underneath her gown. Then she felt his fingers at the opening of her drawers and remembered David lifting himself up on his other elbow, fumbling with the fastenings on his breeches before turning back to her. *I will try to be gentle,* he had mumbled. Sophia groaned out loud, closing her eyes as a wave of acute regret for her actions on that day settled like an iron grid inside her chest.

She didn't comprehend what David planned until he lifted her skirts. She supposed she could have protested at that moment, and he would have stopped. She recalled thinking he would be her husband. It was not wrong to allow him such intimate liberties.

After waiting several weeks for David's return to speak to her father and discuss their eventual marriage, she secured a newssheet from London that carried an announcement of David's betrothal with another woman. At that grave, heart-wrenching moment, she understood she had paid the ultimate price by giving herself to a disloyal man. A week later when her courses started, she experienced sincere gratification to be spared the additional indignity of giving birth to a bastard child.

Now she needed to face the present and the quandary of her puzzling reaction to Sir Edward's kisses. Why did he have the ability to stir the cold, banked fires of her passions when those raw, bruised emotions had lain dormant for so long?

A chilly breeze pulled at loose strands of her hair. She looked up at the sky. Dark, gray clouds scuttled by overhead. Standing up and wrapping her shawl tightly across her shoulders, she strode up the hill toward the back of the house.

"Lady Sophia! I wish to speak to you." Sir Edward rode across the upper pathway in the push chair as John guided him from behind. Peter directed their forward progress in front.

"John, Peter, go find something to do in the stables for a time," he ordered.

"What is it?" she asked as the two men walked away, impatient to return to her room, far away from his unsettling presence.

"I wanted to tell you I am sorry," he replied.

She could feel the fiery, red blush coursing across her cheeks. She forced herself to speak. "I am not surprised. It is distressing to embrace an unrefined, tainted woman such as I."

He gasped. "I am not remorseful for the kisses we shared. It was a wondrous experience that I will always remember and cherish. Rather, I regret securing such gratification from you when I have the knowledge of your past abhorrent, emotional experience."

"Oh." She paused, mentally reviewing his comments with surprise. "Did I understand you correctly, you used the word *wondrous*?"

"Yes, truly extraordinary, as a matter of fact." He grinned at her.

"When…when you wrenched away," she halted, considering her next words. "I thought you were disgusted."

"Never!" His brilliant green eyes widened. "It is my turn to question your choice of words. The embrace brought me great pleasure and delight. Nothing regarding you could ever be cause for revulsion."

"Thank you." Feeling humbled and bewildered, she forced herself to smile.

"I want you to understand," he paused, studying her, "I will always be your friend. After we both leave here, if you ever need my assistance, no matter how trifling, please write to me at Horsham House."

"Oh!" She savored the novelty of being the recipient of his sincere, caring manner, and experienced a warm, tingling sensation in the region of her heart. She couldn't come up with an ingenious reply.

"I greatly admire the intention to set up your own household," he continued. "I comprehend the great struggle and obstacles a woman must overcome when she determines to claim her independence and not marry. I applaud your tenacity."

"I appreciate your generous words and your faith in my abilities. I am considering how best to tell my family of my plans."

"I advise you to secure your living arrangements before speaking to them," he remarked. "You will need to engage a companion as well."

She frowned. "Are you saying I should let a house in London without my father's knowledge?"

"Yes. I am guessing your family would forbid you from following through on the contemplation if you approached them with a representation of your plans initially. Do you have the funds needed to let a cottage or small house?"

"I...I believe so." She pondered on the probable sum required.

"Is there an elderly relation with no family of her own who could be asked to reside with you?"

"I have an unmarried cousin in her forties living in Bath and an elderly aunt, one of my father's sisters, with no other family in Canterbury."

"Both sound like good prospects," he assured her. "Letting a small house in London would cost approximately twenty pounds per year. Of course, you will need a few servants. A footman, cook, and a housemaid. The price of coal runs about forty pounds yearly for a modest residence. If you could afford the additional cost of a coach and two horses requiring a coachman to drive, wages for all the help would run about seventy pounds a year and sixty-five pounds yearly for care of the animals and upkeep on the carriage."

"My goodness!" Her head spun with various sums. "I require approximately five hundred pounds yearly then?"

"At a minimum," he advised. "I believe eight hundred to one thousand pounds yearly would see you settled quite comfortably. Remember you will be required to feed and house the servants as well as yourself and your companion."

"A coach and horses are a luxury I do not believe I could afford," she told him with a frown. "Stables and rooms for the coachman and groom to sleep would mean a larger house and additional letting costs."

"Not necessarily," he rejoined. "If there are mews close by, you can pay a fee to keep a coach and horses there. Learn what the choices and costs are before deciding against keeping a vehicle. I could write to my banker in London and ask him to look into available homes."

"Thank you for your offer, but I must decline. I would not presume upon you to do such a thing for me."

"I assure you it is not an imposition," he assured her. "It only requires my request for the information. I will say my mother and sister are interested in acquiring their own abode if it would make you more comfortable."

"Very well." She studied him. "You are quite knowledgeable of the various aspects of owning a house in London."

"Do I shock you with the breadth of my understanding?" He chuckled. "I own a townhouse on Charles Street in Mayfair just down from Berkeley Square."

She gasped. "You do?"

"Yes. I visit London a few times a year. My mother and sister spend several months there. It made sense to purchase a house we could all live in when we stay in the city."

"How very wonderful and convenient. I remember Camille mentioning her visits to London when we were in finishing school together. I assumed she stayed with an older relative."

"Perhaps my mother and sister could accompany you on your search for a residence," he suggested. "I am certain they plan to return to London soon."

"Your mother has very good reason not to think kindly of me after I took the liberty of inviting Sir Raeford to the party last summer without her prior consent," she reminded him, turning away to stare at some stalks of green beans growing at the edge of the kitchen garden. "I have no idea how much longer I will be sequestered here."

"Ah, yes, I forgot that awkward occasion and your indefinite sojourn," he sighed. "Here come John and Peter to escort me back to my room. I admit I am weary."

She whirled around to face him. "Oh, I am sorry! I should not have kept you talking for so long."

He grinned at her. "You mistake the matter. I requested your attendance and gladly participated in the discussion. Do not forget, we are friends. If you ever need anything, get in touch with me."

"I will remember. Thank you." She trained her gaze on the back of his head as the two men pushed him away from her, down the long pathway to the house.

Chapter Fourteen

He woke from a nap and lay back against the pillows, staring fixedly at the ceiling. It had proved to be a day of great significance. After so many hours spent lying in bed, he finally procured a special treat, a ride in the push chair. It had provided him with the ability to fill his lungs with precious, brisk outdoor air. Then the experience inside the wondrous conservatory, the lush trees, and blooming flowers, as well as an exotic pineapple. The most glorious event in all, was something not planned: the kiss he shared with Lady Sophia.

A sudden gasp escaped from his mouth as he comprehended a sense of intense regret for the embrace. A jarring sensation indeed, to seize such a monumental, exciting occasion one moment, and apprehend broad sorrow the next. What had come over him? Lady Sophia's experience in her youth marked her as someone never to be trifled with, yet he had captured her lips within his own, giving no thought to anything other than a brief dalliance. This fact surely made him no better than her lover at sixteen. Thankfully, there was his sterling reputation regarding previous affairs with a few lonely widows, certainly a steadfast example of his aboveboard dealings with women. He hoped the spontaneous embrace wouldn't cause Lady Sophia to hesitate to act upon the offer of his friendship and aid, should she require it in the future.

"Sir Edward! Did the push chair accomplish all I promised?" Mrs. Canning stood smiling at him from the doorway, with her young son at her side.

"Yes! Yes, it did. It was wonderful to be out of the house!"

She moved inside the room. Her son followed, gripping her skirts. "No problems getting out of bed or handling the contraption?"

"No, no, not at all. The surgeon recruited several men for the complicated business of lifting me into the chair. John took on the operation of the rolling cart most efficiently. Peter made certain the pathways ahead of us were clear of any obstacles," he assured her.

"Did you go fast, sir?" inquired Charles, peeking out from behind his mother.

He laughed, albeit with a grim edge. "I am not such a dare devil, young man. I certainly do not want to reinjure my leg."

"It would be a great pity if such a horrible thing happened," acknowledged Mrs. Canning. "I am very glad to hear you enjoyed a nice outing outside. Do you need anything else at the moment?"

"As a matter of fact, I wanted to make a request. My estate secretary has a knack for tinkering and mechanics. If you would permit me to draw a rough sketch of the chair and its wheels to send to him? I plan to instruct him to have one built for my own use. I feel it is important for me to continue to take these short excursions until I can walk again."

"What an extremely good notion! I will ask Hendrik to bring you the necessary materials. But surely you do not plan to leave us so soon?"

He frowned. "Mr. Gordon believes I will be required to keep my leg elevated for three more weeks. I cannot stay here indefinitely trespassing on your hospitality. He agreed I may travel home safely in my coach next week."

She studied him with furrowed brows. "Please do not rush off and risk further injury. You are quite welcome to stay as long as necessary."

"Thank you very much, Mrs. Canning. I promise not to leave before I can make the attempt safely."

"Very well. I must be satisfied with that assurance. Please rest. I will see you at dinner." She reached down to smooth her son's wavy locks. "Come along, Charles."

"Good-bye, sir!" called the lad as he whipped around and sprinted out of the room into the hallway.

"Good-bye!" He gripped his hands together on his lap staring down at his thumbs. Certainly it was a much more desirable proposition to complete his recovery in the comfort of his own home. It was galling to be dependent on others for food and shelter. Thank goodness Hawkes had arrived to see to his personal needs.

Hendrik entered the room a few minutes later, holding paper, pencil, and a slim volume tucked under his arm. "I took the liberty of trimming both points for you, sir."

He sat up against the pillows, reaching for the instrument and paper. "Thank you."

"I apprehended you might require something to write on as well." The butler held up the slim portfolio before placing it on his lap.

"Good thinking, Hendrik. I trust the book is not

one of great value? I would hate to harm it in my present state of awkward clumsiness."

"No, sir. I discussed my notion with Mrs. Canning," the butler assured him. "She recommended this volume on local bird life in the area. It is lightweight, making the book easier for you to maneuver."

He casually flipped through the first few pages, noting bits of texts combined with detailed, colored drawings. "I will treat it with care, regardless. Please bring the push chair a little closer to the bed before you go."

"Yes. Of course, sir." Hendrik moved to do his bidding. "Will there be anything else?"

"Not at the moment, thank you." He bent over the paper to write the heading *Moving Chair* at the top.

"Hello!"

He looked up from the paper to see Lady Sophia standing in the doorway. "Good afternoon."

"Are you busy?"

"I am attempting to create a detailed image of the chair," he informed her. "Tell me, do you have a talent for illustration?"

She scowled as she strolled into the room to stand by the bed. "No, drawing was never my strong suit. The headmistress at school often lamented my *crooked lines and wobbly people.*"

"Ha!" He lowered the pencil to study her. "I imagine you excelled in embroidery?"

"No, not at all," she countered. "I suppose I performed marginally better only because I learned to follow the outlines on the samplers. I never drew worthy marks on a blank canvas."

"I understand. I will certainly not ask for your assistance."

"Are you intending to retain the drawing of the chair as a keepsake?" she questioned with a grin.

He glared at her before inquiring, "You believe it will serve as a warning to me if I ever think to ride my horse on deserted lanes in extremely bad weather again?"

She giggled, obviously unconcerned with his peevishness. "I am deservedly chastened. Merely a way to pass the time before dinner, then?"

"I plan to send the sketch to my secretary," he grumbled and then cleared his throat. "He has a talent for building contraptions. It is my hope he will finish a similar chair for my use when I return home next week."

"You are leaving?" She reached out to grip his arm and stared down at him, her violet-hued eyes glowing.

"I cannot stay here for days on end invading your aunt's home, causing extra work for her and her servants," he clarified in a stern manner, hoping to suppress any doubts about his upcoming departure. "Mr. Gordon estimates I will need to keep my leg elevated at least three more weeks."

"Horsham must be forty miles away. It cannot be safe for you to travel so far in a carriage!"

"My estate is approximately forty-five miles from here. My coach is well-sprung. The seats are padded with soft supple, leather embellished with petit point cushions. I asked Hawkes to procure something adequate to rest my leg on. I plan to leave early in the morning, taking the normally seven-hour trip in easy stages. Every conceivable option for my comfort has been addressed."

"Mr. Gordon agrees a long journey will not compromise your injury in any way?" She continued to clutch his arm.

He nodded. "One needs to acknowledge the risk of an accident anytime we travel. If such a horrible event should happen to take place on my journey, there will certainly be additional problems to concern myself with."

"Yet you are willing to take that gamble in order to return home?"

He dropped the pencil and put his hand on top of hers, gently squeezing it. "Each of us tempt fate whenever we climb into a carriage. Does it stop us from traveling? I will miss you as well. Your entertaining, stimulating conversation saved me from infinite boredom."

She stepped backward, breaking contact. "I did not mention yearning for your presence after you are gone!"

He raised his brows at her agitated tone. "Perhaps I misjudged the extent of our affinity? I understood we had forged a rapport or a pact together. Am I wrong?"

She avoided his gaze, instead staring down at the floor. "No, you are correct. Forgive me. I wonder if I can ever be comfortable in my new guise."

"You are no longer playing a role. This is not a pretense," he reminded her. "After so many years hiding your true character, it is not surprising you would occasionally slip back into the false demeanor. I advise you to remember something. Be self-confident and not self-centered. Your uniqueness will shine for all to see and appreciate."

She looked up, silently contemplating him. "Thank you. I…I am ashamed and humbled by your words. I admit never giving a thought to the consequences my falsehoods would cause to others as well as myself."

"Wretched situations require desperate measures," he acknowledged. "Perhaps unconsciously, we adapt in ways best suited for our survival at the time."

"Yes. I agree with your statement. Not being required to address the painful tangibility of a betrothal to a man I have no feelings for simply because my parents deem him worthy, brought me much comfort over the years," she admitted.

"And now setting up a household of your own will bring additional solace," he replied, with a smile.

"I…I wished to ask your opinion. I thought to request Sir Raeford to accompany me on my search for lodgings. My maid will be in attendance as well."

"Ah, I had forgotten Sir Raeford." He studied her with half-closed eyes. "Remind me. What is your relationship with him?"

"He is a friend. He is also a convenient companion at balls and parties, when I require the ability to check or dampen other gentleman's potential interest."

He glared at her. "He is a true contender for your hand?"

"No, of course not! He told me repeatedly he has no intention of ever marrying."

"Indeed." He paused for a moment as he contemplated her comments about the gentleman. "Regardless, there will come a time in the future when he understands the need to secure an heir to his property."

She acknowledged his statement with a nod.

"Possibly. However, that requirement need not concern me. Returning to my previous query, do you believe Sir Raeford should help me secure a house in London?"

"I assume he keeps his own lodgings there?" he inquired. "He is familiar with acceptable letting cost, supplies, and servant fees?"

"Oh, yes! He is forever lamenting the high cost of coal and brandy."

"Two extremely important commodities," he agreed. "If you feel you can trust his assessment, I do not see why you shouldn't ask for his advice. I would offer my assistance, but I imagine you wish to begin searching for a residence as soon as possible."

"I must first await a summons from my father to return to London, of course."

"Surely Lord Breech does not plan to keep you hidden away here for many more weeks?"

She shrugged her shoulders. "Perhaps...perhaps I will write to him and inquire."

"A good idea." He picked up the discarded pencil and resumed his sketch. "Sir Raeford should be apprised of your plans as well."

"You are correct." She walked toward the doorway. "I will write to both of them immediately."

"Until dinner then," he called out, pausing his drawing to study her retreating form, fervently wishing he could stand on his own two legs.

Chapter Fifteen

When Sophia reached her bedchamber, she walked over to the small desk in the corner of the room, pulling two sheets of foolscap from the top drawer. Sitting down on the chair, she reached for the goose quill pen, checking the nub before dipping the instrument into the jar of ink.

She glanced outside at the view of the side garden from her window, as she contemplated how to approach the letter to her father. Surely the fierce anger he directed at her as a result of the misunderstanding at the Covington ball had abated? Perhaps the best method would be to adopt a direct course of action and simply ask to come home. While she enjoyed spending time here with her aunt, she longed to return to London. She missed strolling in the parks, visiting the museums, and conversing with friends. Because Mr. Hoover allowed her to use his back office to fill the orders, the process of mixing, packing, and delivery of her face lotion went much more smoothly from town as well. Of course, the desire to secure a home of her own brought additional thoughts of wistfulness. While eager to begin the search, she recognized the wisdom of Sir Edward's opinion to keep her plans secret until she found an ideal dwelling.

She quickly composed the letter, managing to stay deliberately vague. After assuring her father of her own well-being and inquiring as to the state of his and her mother's health, she finished the missive with a brief, polite request to be informed when she may be allowed to return home. Sir Raeford's note also proved a simple matter to complete. After mentioning she hoped he arrived safely back from his recent journey to Paris, she asked him to be ready to accompany her on an unusual shopping exhibition upon her return to London in the near future. She would wait on the matter of obtaining a companion until she got back to town. She signed, folded, sealed, and addressed each letter before taking them downstairs.

Hendrik stood at his post in the front hall.

"Please see these go out today."

"Of course, my lady. This came for you a few minutes ago." He handed her a folded note with her name scrawled on the front.

"Thank you." She noted the familiar handwriting of the chemist Mr. Hoover. She quickly tugged the seal open, reading the contents. He had a few additional orders for her lotion. Advantageously, she had left a good bit of rice kernels soaking in lemon juice in the gardener's shed yesterday. It would be an easy matter to finish the grinding process and fill some jars. She stuffed the note in her pocket and turned toward the stairs, intending to go to her bedchamber and change into another gown.

"Sophia! May I have a word with you?" Aunt Joan called out from the hallway.

"Yes, of course." She paused, with one foot on the first stair.

Her aunt glanced at her butler, occupied with straightening a portrait of Mr. Canning in the entry.

"Perhaps it would be best if we have our conversation in your room."

"Very well. Is something the matter?" She wrapped her hand around her aunt's arm, and they ascended the stairs together.

"No, my dear, nothing is wrong," her aunt replied, smiling.

Reassured, she led the way to her bedchamber and opened the door. "Come in."

"I wished to inquire if Sir Edward informed you that he plans to leave soon." She strolled across the carpeted floor to sit on the love seat in front of the fireplace.

Sophia took a place next to her. "Yes. He told me. I managed to obtain a promise from him. He will not travel until Mr. Gordon informs him it is safe to do so."

"I understand he sent to his estate for his coach with the luxurious interior," her aunt mused. "He should be quite comfortable on the journey back. I wondered if perhaps a traveling companion would be of benefit to him as well."

She frowned, not understanding the implication. "Are you referring to his valet? I believe he will ride inside the coach with him. Someone must see to the proper positioning of his injured leg."

"I thought perhaps you could ride with him," she clarified, adding, "I don't mean to sound as if I am asking you to leave, my dear. I have greatly enjoyed your visit. But surely you don't plan to stay here tucked away from London and your society friends much longer?"

"I go with him?"

"Yes. Naturally, your maid would accompany you.

Your coach could follow and be used to transport additional trunks as well as his valet," her aunt determined. "Your conversation would keep Sir Edward's mind off his injury and make the journey appear shorter. Of course, it would require an additional day of travel for you to return to London."

"You place too much faith in my ability to keep Sir Edward entertained with my discourse, Aunt," she countered. "We would be at daggers drawn before too many miles had been covered."

She chuckled. "I believe you have too little assurance in your own resourcefulness, my dear."

Sophia pondered her aunt's notion before informing her, "I sent a letter to my father just this morning inquiring when I will be able to return to London."

"It is a matter for him to decide, then?"

"My unseemly behavior at the ball prompted my father's decision to send me here for a visit," she explained. "It follows, I must wait until he has forgiven my lapse in judgement and granted me leave to return home."

"I don't wish to sound overbearing, but isn't the punishment rather high-handed for the transgression?" Aunt Joan questioned with a frown. "As I understand it, the unfortunate episode occurred accidentally."

"You are correct," she replied. "I believe the crux of the matter is my overall attitude. Father is intent on securing an advantageous marriage for me. He views every social event I attend as a cause for hope. I am a continual disappointment to him in this regard. The muddle at the Covington ball proved to be the breaking point. He is no longer able to tolerate my failure to secure a suitor."

"You are purposely avoiding marriage, dear," her aunt pointed out. "Although I still hope one day you would find a man to love, surely it is time to explain the root cause of the shirking away from their wishes to your family?"

She sighed, pausing to look out the window and study the trees waving gently in the breeze. "I suppose I must. No matter what the circumstances of my past, it will not be a simple matter to make them understand why I would choose to live the rest of my life as a spinster."

"No, it will not be easy," she acknowledged. "But with understanding comes acceptance. Once your family has come to terms with your desires, they will allow you to begin to fashion and construct your own destiny."

"I trust you are right, Aunt." She turned to smile at her. "I promise to confront them soon after I return home."

"Good. Let me know when you hear from your father." She stood up and smoothed the wrinkles from her skirt. "I must check on Charles. His tutor informed me yesterday he far surpassed his expectations for him in Latin. He asked if I would bring by one of my botany books containing the species names in that language to further challenge Charles."

"My goodness, perhaps he requires more intensive instruction?"

"It certainly appears so," Aunt Joan agreed as she walked to the door. "I must write to George and ask his opinion. Please broach the matter of accompanying Sir Edward home to him. I will see you later, my dear."

Sophia pulled the note from the chemist from her pocket after her aunt left and rang for her maid. She helped her to change out of her morning gown and don a well-worn garment, one saved to wear when concocting her solution. She sat down at the make-up table. While Josephine brushed the tangles from her hair, she stared at her reflection in the mirror, pondering her aunt's suggestion. Should she make the offer to accompany Sir Edward to his home? Would it be presumptuous of her?

"Finished, my lady." Josephine tucked one wayward curl in a hairpin before stepping away.

"Thank you." She patted the tightly woven braid on the crown of her head before picking up the list. "I received additional orders from Mr. Hoover. Please bring me eight vials. I will affix the labels to the jars, address the crate here, and be in the garden shed if anyone asks for me."

"Very well, my lady," her maid answered, going to the closet and removing the carefully wrapped glass containers from the trunk. She placed them next to her on the table before leaving the room, closing the door behind her.

Sophia copied the names from Mr. Hoover's list onto wafer-sized disks of parchment. After lighting her taper, she slowly dripped the softened wax onto the backs of each of the labels and then attached them, one by one, to the vials. Cutting soft linen into short strips, she wrapped the material around each jar and placed the containers into the small crate lined with more pieces of linen. After securing the lid, she wrote Mr. Hoover's address on the top.

She stood up from the table, quickly walking out of

her room. Striding down the hallway to the back stairs, she reached the kitchen without encountering anyone else. With a brisk nod to Cook, she hastened outside and followed the well-worn path rounding the corner of the kitchen garden.

"Where are you going in such a hurry?" Sir Edward inquired with a smug expression, from his chair parked in front of the shed.

"Oh!" Her precipitous attempt to bring herself from a forward stride to a sudden halt proved futile. She lunged forward, only just managing to grip the arm of the push chair with one hand, averting disaster. "You startled me!"

"Are you hurt?" He reached out to grip her wrist.

"No, I am fine," she assured him as she pushed against the contraption, using it as leverage to stand up straight again. "Why are you here?"

He sighed. "I completed my drawing and needed some fresh air. I had a query for Mr. Grimmer pertaining to rose cultivation."

She frowned at him, tucking the crate behind her back. "I see. Did he answer your question?"

"John couldn't locate the man," he replied. "I told him to leave me here in the cool shade. I hope to catch Mr. Grimmer before he goes home for the day."

"Oh." She stared at the ground pondering her next move. Should she excuse herself, turn around and return to the house, or nonchalantly enter the shed and prepare her mixture?

"Do you have business with him?"

"Excuse me?" His query brought her resolute deliberation to a standstill.

"Do you have a question for Mr. Grimmer as

well?"

She contemplated the situation. What to do? Sir Edward knew of her other secrets. Why should the existence of her cosmetic be kept from him? Would he think her foolish? He advised her to be honest in dealings with others. She quickly resolved to take the chance on his sanction of her unique activity. "I have secured a bit of counter space in the shed from Mr. Grimmer to concoct my face lotion."

"Face lotion!"

"Shhh!" She put a finger to her lips, glancing toward the house. "My aunt has no knowledge of this."

"Sir, are you ready for me to take you back to your room?" John asked as he walked toward them.

"No, not yet," he told him, before turning back to her. "Would you care to elaborate?"

"Wait a moment. Don't go, John," she called out, as her coachman turned away. She pointed to the raised sill on the floor in the shed's doorway. "I need your assistance. Could you manage to maneuver the chair across the threshold?"

"Yes, of course, my lady." John got behind the contraption and gripped the bar at the back. "Hold tight, sir!"

"Make certain my leg doesn't slip off the plank!"

"Let me go inside first," she advised. "I will insure nothing goes awry."

The front wheel didn't touch the ground as John pushed forward, using only the rear ones. Once across the protruding sill, he lifted the chair from the back using the front wheels as leverage. He guided the contraption to a stop just inside the door. "No harm done, sir?"

"Thank you. I am still in one piece," Sir Edward replied with a sigh. His hand shook as he smoothed back a lock of hair that had fallen across his forehead.

"I have a few more orders, John," she informed her coachman. "It shouldn't take very long to fill the vials and pack the crate. Come back in about twenty minutes. I will have it ready for you. Please leave the door open."

"Very well, my lady." He turned and walked outside.

She reached for her apron, tying it behind her back before facing Sir Edward. "I don't have much time. I will explain as I go."

"Stop a moment. How did this come about and why?"

"Allow me to attend to this first." She put a piece of parchment on the counter before picking up the container with the rice soaking in the lemon juice. She strained the liquid from some of the kernels with a piece of cheesecloth and dropped them into her Wedgwood mortar. Then she gripped the wooden pestle, placing it against the softened rice and began grinding back and forth across the hard porcelain surface. "My childhood nurse had a large, purple birthmark across a cheek just below one eye. To hide the blemish, she applied Gowland's Lotion over a period of several years. No one advised her that it contained a mercuric chloride corrosive combined with toxic acid. A top layer of skin can fall off if the cosmetic is used regularly for any length of time. Her birthmark became inflamed and her skin pitted. Just before she learned the true extent of the lotion's hazards, she began to lose her sight in the eye and paralysis set in across the one side of her body. She left me when I had just turned ten years old, passing away in great pain in her sister's home a few months later."

"I am sorry," he murmured. "That is a terrible manner in which to die."

She pressed the few remaining hard bits of rice kernels against the side of the mortar. "The image of her damaged complexion haunted me throughout my childhood. As I grew older, I made a vow to experiment with only natural ingredients and produce a product that would never cause harm to a woman's skin or bring other horrific conditions. Shortly after I returned from finishing school, I discovered women in Japan used rice flour to accomplish smooth, even skin tone and uniform opaque complexion."

"How did you learn of the Japanese method?"

She spooned the smooth paste into another bowl, slowly mixing in the olive oil. "Initially, I understood I required basic knowledge of the ingredients commonly used in lotions and creams. One day while shopping with my maid, I found a small chemist's shop on the edge of Mayfair. I went inside and asked the proprietor several questions. When he observed the extent of my engagement on the subject, he kindly agreed to tutor me in the process if I would give him a small amount of the money I hoped to eventually earn from my potion. A book Mr. Hoover had on the cosmetics used by the Geisha of Gion in Kyoto, Japan further sparked my interest. It described the women's use of rice powder as a natural emollient to achieve soft, pearly-white skin tone. It also protects from sun damage and prevents wrinkles."

"You found the pure component you were looking

for!"

She finished the mixing process before glancing at him. He stared at her with raised brows obviously waiting for her to comment. "Are you amused?"

"Are you asking if I believe you are foolish for dabbling in the world of commerce? Certainly not! I am quite impressed." His voice resounded with notes of sincerity. "What do you call your creation?"

Her cheeks warmed as she replied, "Lady's Lotion."

"Ha! Wonderful! Quite suitable," he chuckled. "How much do you charge per vial? I wish to purchase two, one for Mother and one for Camille."

"No!" she hastily turned away, grabbing the crate and pulling out the labeled bottles. "They must not know of this! All my customers retrieve the solution from Mr. Hoover's shop. They believe he is the creator."

He didn't reply. She ignored him, concentrating on her process, holding the end of her silver funnel over the first bottle with one hand and pouring the mixture with the other.

"Could I offer my assistance?"

His abrupt query startled her. The hand holding the bowl shook and a bit of the lotion splashed onto the counter. "Oh, no!"

"What happened?"

"I dropped some of the mixture." She put the bowl down and hastily wiped the spill with a piece of cloth. Thankfully, she had used the parchment paper. There would be no trace of a stain.

"I apologize. I am good for nothing in the state I'm in!"

"There is no call for you to chastise yourself," she admonished, as she quickly filled the rest of the vials. "I have more than enough remaining lotion to suffice."

He exhaled a deep breath. "I am greatly comforted to hear that."

She put the stoppers in the bottles and packed them carefully inside the crate with some of the pieces of material wrapped around each one. Closing the box, she glanced at the chemist's address, making certain the ink hadn't smudged and was still legible. She washed her hands at the sink, wiped off the bowl, mortar and pestle, putting them on a shelf, before tugging off the apron and facing him. "Do you understand why my involvement in this must remain a secret?"

"Yes. I suppose society would be a harsh assessor if it were to become generally known." He frowned. "I acknowledge the great impetuous to create the cosmetic, but once you came up with the solution, why did you not allow Mr. Hoover to carry on with subsequent development of it? I assume he deals with the order process and the customers?"

She caught her bottom lip between her teeth and turned away, contemplating the garden view from the doorway, as she deliberated her answer. "I suppose you could call it a need for self-worth. I previously alluded to my lack of capability in other *womanly* talents. My musical abilities are similarly poor. Even though I can never take credit for inventing the mixture, I experience a sense of great pride in my accomplishment and continue to do so with every vial of lotion I fill."

"Admirable. Will you please look at me?"

She slowly turned around to face him. "Yes?"

"I meant what I said. I am impressed and very

pleased to know you completed your experiments despite the hardships certainly caused along the way, because you are female. You were able to create the thing you vowed to do. You continued on, eventually achieving success." He grinned at her. "You don't give up very easily, do you?"

"No," she acknowledged with a hesitant smile. "Not if it is something I am passionate about."

"Hmmm." A smug expression swept across his face. "I would be interested in knowing what else can cause you to respond so fervently."

"Are you ready to go back to your chamber, sir?"

Thankfully, the abrupt sound of her coachman's voice brought her back to her senses. She had almost blurted the words, *your kiss*. Utterly dismayed, she made a sudden movement toward the doorway, thrusting the crate into John's hands. "See that this gets on the next mail coach to London. I will see you later, Sir Edward."

Chapter Sixteen

Hendrik held out chairs for both Sophia and Mrs. Canning at the table in Sir Edward's chamber later that evening.

"Thank you. You may pour the wine now, Hendrik. What did you think of my suggestion, Sir Edward?"

"Your suggestion? To what are you referring, Mrs. Canning?"

"Sophia?"

"I am sorry, Aunt." She cringed, as her cheeks flushed rosily. "It slipped my mind."

Mrs. Canning frowned at her before she looked at him. "I advised Sophia you would greatly benefit from a companion on the journey back to your estate."

He smiled at her. "Thank you for your concern. Are you forgetting my valet, Hawkes? He accompanies me to ensure proper repose of my injured leg. While certainly not the consummate conversationalist, he will provide me with ample discourse to see me through to the journey's end."

"You misunderstand." Mrs. Canning took a sip of her wine. "I am recommending my niece accompany you on the trip."

His mouth cleaved open in surprise and his brows drew together on his forehead. "Lady Sophia?"

"Yes. I assured my niece I enjoyed her visit and have no intention of forcing her to leave, but I have no doubt she is eager to return to London," she explained as a servant put a bowl of soup in front of her. "This is an opportunity she should not miss. The additional coach could be used to carry trunks and bags as well as your valet. Sophia and her maid would ride with you."

He drank deeply from his wine glass before turning to gaze at Lady Sophia. "What is your reaction to your aunt's proposition?"

She shrugged her shoulders and picked up her soup spoon before answering. "I hesitate to reply, not wishing to sound pompous. If you believe my company on the journey would make the travel less tedious for you, I will gladly accompany you. However, as I previously explained to my aunt, I cannot leave her care until I have my father's permission to do so."

"There is that thorny issue to be resolved first, of course." He raised his arms to allow a servant to place a tray of food in front of him.

"I will take the journey only if you truly wish for me to come along." She avoided his gaze, bending over to sip the broth from her bowl.

"Our repartee would offer a decided improvement over Hawkes' grumblings," he affirmed and arched an eyebrow. "I must point out that you go several miles out of your way and must stay the night at Horsham House. The circumstance should be of no inconvenience. My mother and Camille will be there for another fortnight. I believe Miss Cather is visiting as well."

"Oh, yes. Lady Collins mentioned her before she left. I…I understood her family to be residing in London for the season," Lady Sophia pointed out as she slowly lowered her spoon to the table.

"You are correct. They rarely miss a season." He picked up his fork, glaring absentmindedly at the mashed bits of food on his plate. "Mother insinuated she would be good company for my…my sister."

"I sense a mother's hand in an attempt to promote a match," Mrs. Canning observed. A servant took away her empty soup bowl and placed a small dish covered with sliced pheasant, potatoes, and carrots in front of her.

He winced as he dropped the fork onto the tray with a loud clatter. "I apologize. I am inordinately clumsy this evening."

"Do you welcome Miss Cather's presence in your home?" Mrs. Canning inquired. "Are you anxious to further your acquaintance with her?"

His gallant attempt at changing the subject hadn't worked. "Not at all. My sister enjoys her companionship. I imagine my mother hoped the two girls would entertain each other while I finish my convalescence."

"Miss Cather is an exceptionally fine reader," Lady Sophia commented before taking another sip of her wine and then picking up her fork. "She often read to us in the evenings at finishing school. You must request her to narrate *Othello* to you. Recalling Miss Cather's desperate tone as she recited Desdemona's pleading words begging Othello to spare her life still causes my pulse to race and my heart to squeeze in anguish."

"I…I will remember your endorsement," he remarked, wondering why she would recommend him listening to such a heartbreaking tale when the situation he found himself in already made him overly despondent. He glanced at her, observing her full lips curling upward. "You dare to provoke me, my lady?"

"Yes," she admitted with a grin. "I find it amusing when you struggle to maintain a semblance of polite dignity when taking part of a discussion you clearly wish had never begun in your presence."

"Botheration!" He bent over the tray to put a bite of mashed potato mixed with chopped pieces of pheasant into his mouth.

"The current spirited dialogue between you both illustrates my point succinctly," observed Mrs. Canning as she pushed aside her empty dish. "I am glad we agreed to a light meal this evening, Sophia. The substantial tea we had together this afternoon left me with little appetite."

"I certainly ate more than my share of Cook's delicious lemon tarts," she concurred.

"I will relay your approbation to her," Mrs. Canning answered, with a smile. "I wish to repeat what I stated previously, the day-long journey to your estate would be much more entertaining if my niece accompanied you, Sir Edward."

He lowered the fork onto his barren plate, reclining back against the pillows with a sigh. "I must warn you. I cannot promise to remain on my best behavior cooped up inside the carriage for so many hours."

Lady Sophia choked on a laugh and covered her mouth with her serviette. "Are you saying you have been a paragon the entire duration of your stay here? What are you like when you consider yourself a nuisance? I seem to remember you were aloof and withdrawn at the house party last summer."

Her observations forced him to reflect on his sour disposition on full display much of the time since he had arrived at her aunt's home. The gathering the previous summer had been inflicted on him very suddenly without prior notice by his mother. Discomfited by his ruminations and Lady Sophia's amusement at his expense, he lashed out without first deliberating his words, "You needn't concern yourself and accompany me. You overplayed your hand taking care of me when I was delirious with the fever. Consider any debt owed paid in full."

The mirth she displayed moments before vanished, and a choking gasp escaped from her mouth. She quickly stood up, dropping her serviette to the table with an unsteady hand. "I...I didn't sleep very well last night. I believe I will retire early."

"Sophia!" Mrs. Canning rose from her seat.

"No. Stay, Aunt." She strode out of the room without turning around.

The sound of her footsteps retreating down the hall gradually faded away. "I am sorry. I will apologize to your niece at the first opportunity."

Mrs. Canning returned to her chair. She contemplated him. "Sparks tend to fly when you two are together."

He grimaced. "I do not understand what comes over me and can't blame my attitude entirely on my injury. I start out intending to tread lightly with her, and then she says something that sets me off, and I speak without thought to the consequences."

"I continue to believe Sophia should accompany you on your journey home."

"Indeed? I am surprised, after the example you just observed."

"It would be of benefit to you both," she answered

with conviction, standing up and strolling to the side of his bed. Two servants entered the room and began clearing away the cutlery, bowls, and plates. "Tell me how many times you noticed the discomfort once the contentious discussion with my niece began tonight?"

"The discomfort?"

"The pains in your leg," she clarified.

"Oh." He paused a moment to deliberate. "Surprisingly, I admit I didn't perceive the ache at all. I only thought of how best to obligate her to stop pretending and say what first came to her mind without prevarication."

"While I believe the harmless squabbles between you aid in breaking the chains she wrapped herself in, you would do well to remember Sophia is now off-balanced. Go gently. She is not accustomed to the sensation. As you are aware, she has managed to rigidly control her temperament as well as the appearance she shows to others since the unfortunate episode several years ago."

"I comprehend what you are saying. I will make it a point not to provoke her again." He clutched the bed sheets and pursed his lips together while he considered how to phrase his next query. "I must inquire, please counsel me, am I wrong to bring up the subject of her care?"

She frowned at him. "You refer to the time Sophia spent here when you first arrived?"

"Yes." He took a deep breath and held it as he waited for her answer.

"I promised her I would not say anything to you on the subject," she replied. "However, now you have learned something of her attentions to you, I consider the promise no longer binding. I believe my niece is apprehensive of you learning how much time she actually spent caring for you."

"I don't understand." He gasped, startled by the underlying significance of her words. "What are you saying?"

Mrs. Canning stood still with her gaze trained on him. "The first two nights Sophia sat at your bedside without leaving until early dawn, only agreeing to allow a servant to take over for her while she went to her room for a few hours to get some rest."

He couldn't speak for several moments. "I am prostrate to hear this. I assumed she only visited for a brief period during the day to check on me and to casually mop my brow."

"Hello, Mrs. Canning, Sir Edward," the surgeon spoke out from the doorway.

"Mr. Gordon, please come in. We have just finished our evening meal. Your patient has learned my niece provided essential care to him in the first days of his illness. You will wish to discuss the particulars with him. I will see you in the morning, Sir Edward."

"I will speak of the occasion only if I have your leave to do so," the surgeon contested, as he stepped back to allow space for Mrs. Canning to walk to the doorway.

"I give my permission." She gripped the door frame before turning away, declaring, "It is past time my niece's diligence is recognized."

Mr. Gordon placed his bag on the floor and walked over to the side of the bed. "How are you feeling?"

"Like I've been jabbed in the face and punched in the gut. Mrs. Canning just clarified how much time

Lady Sophia spent watching over me. Tell me the true importance of the role she played in my recovery."

"She certainly did much more than making an occasional visit to check on your well-being." The surgeon cleared his throat. "It is impossible to say if you would have conquered the fever and improved on your own. You are young, strong, and healthy. However, a severe episode of the sickness has been known to destroy the most stalwart patient. Many believe a sense of companionship in the depths of delirium is beneficial. Also, constant observation of the sick individual, ensuring a lower surface body temperature is maintained, can sometimes bring about a turn for the better in some of the gravest cases. Lady Sophia proved ingenious. She requested chunks of ice wrapped in towels to be placed at your side while the fever raged inside you."

"Are…are you saying," he paused to take a deep breath, "Do you mean to tell me, she could be responsible for saving my life?"

"Yes. It is entirely possible."

"I…I owe her so much!"

"Some words of advice before you say anything to Lady Sophia," the surgeon cautioned. "She pleaded with me not to mention her role in your recovery to you. When I questioned her reticent attitude, she told me she spurned the notion of having an unattached gentleman indebted to her. She further clarified she would never allow herself to be in a position obligated to marry any man."

"Ah…I understand. Thank you for explaining the situation. I will consider what you have told me before I speak with her."

"Good. Do you remain adamant to return to your estate?"

"Yes. I plan to leave here early next week, with your agreement of course. My coach will arrive here tomorrow or the next day. My secretary managed to design and build a push chair for me. He advised me it will be ready for my use when I return."

"Excellent! You will need to take the journey in easy stages." The surgeon smiled at him. "Provided you don't fall out of the bed, get tossed from the push chair, or attempt to waltz, you may travel to your estate next week."

Chapter Seventeen

Sophia slowly opened her eyes the next morning to see the sun streaming in the windows. She raised herself up on one arm, reaching toward the bedside table to clutch her pocket watch and bring it in front of her face to stare at the dials. Nine o'clock! She rarely slept so late!

She placed the watch onto the table, shoved the covers back, and swung her legs over the bed. She stood up, thrusting her feet into her slippers, and tossed her dressing gown across her shoulders when a knock sounded upon the door. "Yes? Come in!"

"You are awake, my lady!" exclaimed Josephine as she strode into the room.

"Yes, I am. Why didn't you call me earlier?"

"Mrs. Canning told me to let you sleep," her maid replied. "She is worried you aren't getting enough rest."

She sighed. "I must admit, my aunt is correct. I haven't been sleeping well."

"Mrs. Canning is a very smart lady," Josephine gushed and then held out two folded pieces of parchment. "These came for you this morning. I am also to tell you Sir Edward wishes to speak with you as soon as you have broken your fast."

Sophia stared at the handwriting on the outside of the missives. The top one addressed to her in Mr. Hoover's handwriting. It most probably contained additional orders. She reached out to set it onto her dressing table while glancing at the other note.

"Oh!" Her stomach heaved as she recognized her father's heavy scrawl. Mr. Hoover's epistle fluttered to the floor. She made her way to a chair in front of the fire, sitting down abruptly as her legs gave way underneath her. She broke the seal with shaking fingers, pulling out the piece of parchment.

Sophia,

I received your letter just as I sat down at my desk to pen a missive to you. You write to ask if you may be allowed to come home. I trust you have used your time away from London in the company of your estimable aunt productively. Your mother and I agree there has been ample opportunity for you to reflect on the untold number of potential suitors you scorned over the years since first making your come-out. It is past time you accept a worthy gentleman and set up your own household. It is my intention to assist you in resolving this matter. I will graciously agree to allow you to return to London on the understanding you are betrothed before your twenty-first birthday, in four months' time. Let us know when we may expect you.

B

As she finished reading, her heart started to pound erratically inside her chest. She gasped as the atmosphere inside her room became stifling, making it hard to breathe. She desperately needed fresh air. She stood up, toppling the chair over backward onto the carpet. Ignoring the capsized piece of furniture, she flung the letter on her dressing table. "Josephine, bring me my yellow morning gown immediately!"

Her maid poked her head out from inside the

connecting dressing room. "Whatever has happened, my lady?"

"Never mind!" She yanked her dressing gown off her shoulders, tossing it onto the bed, and then pulled the nightgown over her head to fling it onto the floor at her feet. "Do as I say!"

Josephine ran to the clothes press, producing the requested garment as well as freshly washed stays and a shift. "Here, my lady."

"Quickly now!" She took a ragged breath as her maid helped her with the undergarments. After those items were in place, she lifted her arms, and her maid guided the gown up over her head. While Josephine fastened the ties and buttons at the back, she adjusted and smoothed the folds in the skirt with her fingers. "Don't bother brushing out my hair. Gather the strands together and secure it in the comb."

"Very well, my lady. I trust it will stay in place. Give me a moment to add some additional pins," her maid advised as she bound her hair tightly and stepped away, tripping over something on the carpet. "What is this? More orders from Mr. Hoover?"

"Oh, yes. I must have dropped it." Sophia took the missive from her and opened the seal, sighing as she read the listed names. "Four more requests. I will return shortly to change and go to the shed to fill the orders."

She grabbed her watch and the note from her father, shoving them in the pocket discreetly tucked in a side pleat in her gown and rushed out of the bedchamber, shutting the door firmly behind her. She quickly strode down the stairs and made her way down the hallway.

"Sophia!" Aunt Joan called to her from the

doorway to the breakfast room. "You are very late today."

"Oh, hello, Aunt," she greeted her with a forced smile.

"Whatever is the matter?" she asked with a frown. "Come, break your fast. I will join you and have some tea."

"I shouldn't. Sir Edward asked for me."

"He is outside sitting in the sun in the push chair." Her aunt reached for the bell pull. "I will ask Hendrik to say you will be joining him shortly. You must eat something first."

"Yes, my lady?" Hendrik inquired from the doorway.

"Please inform Sir Edward that Lady Sophia is breaking her fast. She will attend him when she has finished her meal."

"Very well, my lady." The butler bowed and turned away to walk down the hallway.

"Sit down, my dear." Aunt Joan pulled out a chair. "Here is your tea. What would you like to eat?"

"I am not very hungry. Some eggs and a piece of toast will be fine."

Her aunt spooned some eggs that were kept warm in a warming tray on a side table onto a plate and placed it in front of her. She brought over a basket of toast. "I gave you a piece of bacon as well. Now tell me what is wrong."

"Thank you." Sophia took a gulp of her tea. "I received a reply from my father. He is allowing me to return home."

Aunt Joan smiled. "You will be happy to be back in town and to see your friends again. What has made you so gloomy?"

"He is insisting I am betrothed before I turn twenty-one."

"He what?" she shrieked. "Your birthday is in November, a little over four months from now!"

"That fact matters not to me," she countered. "I have no intention of ever getting married. However, I do wish to return to London. I need your advice. I had resolved to drop the playacting and pretense to become my real self once more. Do I agree to my father's command and pretend for a few more months? Once I turn twenty-one and claim my independence, I will obtain a companion and set up my own household."

Her aunt studied her before speaking. "Sophia, you were deeply hurt when you were sixteen, but there are plenty of good, compassionate men in the world. How wonderful it would be if you could forever banish the pain you carry from the experience in your past and surround yourself with an affectionate, caring family. Is it truly impossible for you to entertain the thought of having a husband and children?"

She gulped the bit of egg she had put in her mouth. "It is not something I could do, Aunt. I greatly admire you and your ability to manage this household, take care of your children, as well as keep up regular correspondence with my uncle who obviously loves you and values your opinion. In my case, young, innocent, and eager to have a home of my own, I fastened onto the first man I met who I believed could grant me all my aspirations and daydreams. After flying so high, the feathers suddenly dropped from my wings, and I fell to the ground. My spirt is crushed, my heart encased in ice forever."

"Oh, Sophia!" Her aunt walked across the room to put a hand on her shoulder. "You are a very lovely, strong young woman. I wish you could find true happiness."

She dropped her fork to her plate and covered Aunt Joan's hand with her own. "Do not worry about me. I am happy and content. I look forward to the experience of securing my own residence in London soon."

"I understand, my dear," she answered, with a tender smile. "I won't say anymore on the subject of marriage. I do think you should drop the role-playing. George told me in his last letter, the crowds of people in London earlier this spring have disappeared. Presumably, most families have returned to their country estates. There shouldn't be too many eligible gentlemen left in the city. Finish your meal and speak with Sir Edward. We will discuss your plans for departure later over our tea."

"Very well." She sighed after Aunt Joan left the room. After gulping down the rest of her tea, she shoved the plate still containing most of the food away to the opposite side of the table. The sour taste of guilt she experienced from not being completely honest with her aunt made her stomach churn. Losing one's virtue wasn't something to speak of to others. It was a sobering thought to realize she had admitted her fatal flaw to Sir Edward. She needed to talk to him. She came to her feet, wiping her mouth with the serviette before tossing it onto her chair.

She strode out of the breakfast room and down the hallway, making her way outside to be immediately soothed by the warm sunshine. After taking a few deep, gulping breaths, she studied the surrounding area and spotted Sir Edward, sitting in the push chair in the shade of the giant elm tree at the edge of the kitchen garden. He frowned at a missive he held in one hand. Not wanting to bother him while he appeared preoccupied with important correspondence, she began to back away when he suddenly raised his head.

His glowing green eyes were murky and opaque. He stared at her for a moment without speaking, as if to place her. "Oh, it is you. Good day."

"Is…Is something wrong?" she called out, quivering as she reluctantly walked toward him, as she recalled her behavior to him the evening before.

He folded up the piece of vellum, stuffing it in his waistcoat pocket. "No, no. My mother writes of an issue on my estate. Never mind that now. Come over here. I wish to apologize for what I said to you last night."

"Apologize? To me?" Her entire body trembled in reaction to his unexpected comment as she slowly lowered herself onto the bench next to him.

"Yes. I acted like a spoiled child. I never should have brought up the subject of your care and thrown it back into your face as if you had done nothing out of the ordinary." He paused, studying her. "With your aunt's concurrence, yesterday I questioned Mr. Gordon about the true extent of your assistance to me. It is his belief that your zealous attendance and endeavors over the first two days and nights could have saved my life."

She forgot her own worries and concerns as she gazed into his eyes, pondering the significance of his words. "My aunt gave him leave to provide you with the details? They both promised me they would not speak of it."

"Come now," he scoffed and reached for her hand. "You knew I guessed you were my devoted nurse. Although the others continually renounced my queries on the subject, you never denied the allegation."

"Please," she begged, her voice hitching on a sob. "Do not feel obligated to offer for me."

"Ah, so that is the cause of your distress." He gently squeezed the tips of her fingers. "Mr. Gordon told me what you said to him. Stop tormenting yourself, my dear. I am deeply grateful for what you did for me. I will always be your friend and ask you for nothing more."

Sophia released the breath she held in one abrupt gush of air. Unconsciously she gripped his hand like a lifeline, rubbing the coarse skin on his knuckles with her thumb. "Th...Thank you! May...May we speak of something else? Your letter...it...it must be a trial to Lady Collins to oversee and make decisions related to your property during your absence."

"Not at all," he answered, releasing her hand. "Since shortly after my father's death six years ago, she has made it her business to continually point out my failings when it comes to running the estate."

"Truly?" She pressed her palms together in her lap noting the grimness of his tone. "Surely you exaggerate?"

"I can assure you I do not overstate the situation." He looked away from her, seemingly to ponder the grass growing underneath his chair. "I...I never mentioned this matter to anyone else."

"I am honored you chose me to confide in," she told him frankly, conscious of a soothing warmth invading the region around her heart.

He sighed deeply and faced her again. "Since I was old enough to remember important events in my daily life, I comprehended I fell short of my father's expectations. I never did well enough in school, my seat on a horse was not up to his standards, I did not bring back the right quantity of dead animals after joining in the hunt, and I certainly could not be relied upon to know the best methods of farming on the family estate."

His tone was despondent. She studied his somber countenance, the fixed, determined set of his mouth, the throbbing vein on his forehead, partially concealed by a wayward lock of hair. The ponderous load of frustration and pain he carried most of his life, because of his parents' lack of trust in his ability to carry on in his father's footsteps became easily discernable. She searched for something to say to ease his sense of worthlessness. "I imagine the eldest or only sons are often held to a higher axiom."

He grunted as he reached down to pull the crumpled piece of vellum out of his pocket. He smoothed out the creases, laying it flat in his lap. "I wish the reasoning could be so lucid. While in London a few weeks ago, I met with a gentleman who is an authority on the benefits of crop rotation, something my father continually refused to attempt. With all that happened, I forgot he planned to visit my estate to see the layout of the crops and advise me further. My mother writes she *informed Mr. Stevens his advice was not required and sent him back to London.* She ends with, *your father taught you the best methods of land management passed down through generations of his family. Surely you cannot think to change such time-honored traditions?* This is one example of the many trials I am continually faced with. The answers are always final. There are no discussions, no questions, never any interest in trying new methods because I couldn't be trusted to fully understand possible ramifications."

"There is an old saying: 'Too many cooks spoil the broth.' Lady Collins must step away and allow you the freedom to make your own decisions. She needs to be confident you will act with the best intentions for your estate and your family," she told him, firmly. "Only in that way can your own talents and creative force become acknowledged."

He chuckled. "Of course, you are right. What a glorious vision your words conjure up! But it will never happen. As long as she lives, my mother will never hand over all the control to me."

She pursed her lips together, frowning at him. "Perhaps Lady Collins needs a distraction, another interest. The season is effectively over. London would offer very few entertainments and amusements at present. Is there an acquaintance she has neglected to visit for a long period of time? Ideally, when you are able to walk again, she needs to leave you on your own for several months so you may begin experimenting and acting upon your ideas."

He sat up straighter in the chair, staring at her with raised brows. "I believe you may have hit upon the answer! My mother has a dear friend in Bath. They were neighbors as children. She often laments not having the time to spare to visit her. She intended to travel there after Camille had contracted a suitor and formal offer of marriage."

"Could your sister be persuaded to travel there with

Lady Collins?" she asked him. "While many elderly people go to Bath in order to drink the waters, surely younger families reside there as well? I have heard of the weekly balls in the Assembly Rooms."

"Yes, of course! I believe Camille would agree to the scheme," he answered with enthusiasm. "You know how compelling she can be when she gets the *bit between her teeth*. Thank you so much for your advice."

She grinned at him. "You are welcome."

"Now to address the subject of your return to London." He tucked the letter back into his waistcoat pocket. "Have you had a reply from Lord Breech?"

"Yes. Yes, I have." She scowled as she reached for the letter. "I wished to speak to you on that very subject."

"I gather from your expression he has not agreed to your return?"

"To the contrary," she retorted. "He informs me he will *graciously allow* my return to the city if I agree to become betrothed before I turn twenty-one in four months' time."

"He…He! No! I cannot believe it!" he bellowed, gripping the arms of the push chair.

"My…my reaction entirely, with a great sense of trepidation as well," she clarified. Her hand trembled as she held out the piece of vellum. "Please read it. He writes in a frantic, veiled tone."

He took the missive from her hand and studied it for several minutes. "I agree. I believe he is hiding something from you. It is entirely within his rights as a father to insist you marry and start a family of your own, but the urgency of his approach is suspect."

"It is imperative I return to London. I need to begin my search for a home to let without delay. I intended to cease all pretenses, but do I dare do so if I am required to present myself to eligible gentlemen immediately upon my return? I discussed the quandary with my aunt. She informed me my uncle had written that the city is quite deserted at present."

He frowned. "You believe any ball or social gathering you might attend would offer an unsubstantial number of prospective suitors? Easily handled without needing to adapt to affectations?"

"Yes."

He did not immediately reply. "I agree, but with some hesitation. The compelling manner of Lord Breech's correspondence makes me concerned he will act on your behalf without due consideration. Be alert to any possible ruse or deceptions."

Chapter Eighteen

Sophia paused just outside the front door. A chilly breeze fanned her cheeks. The early morning summer air had not warmed yet. She scanned the horizon over the tops of the trees lining the drive. A few puffy, white clouds marred the otherwise bright blue sky in the east.

"Make haste, Josephine," she called to her maid who struggled behind her in the entryway to straighten the pile of shawls she carried. They were deemed necessary to bring on the journey to ward off any unexpected, inclement weather.

She descended the stairs, noting Aunt Joan and her nephew Charles stood next to the open door of Sir Edward's carriage.

"Good morning, Sophia," her aunt called out to her as she approached her side. "I promised Charles he could put off his studies today to observe Sir Edward's placement inside the coach."

"Oh yes," she replied with a smile. "I admit I too am curious to see how it will be accomplished."

"It has already been done," commented a voice from inside the vehicle. "See for yourself."

"Sir Edward?" She peered inside the dim interior.

"The footmen and grooms were bang up to the mark!" Charles jumped up and down on one foot.

"Charles! Where did you learn such language?" admonished his mother.

"Sorry, mum," he muttered.

"You were caught up in the excitement of the moment and forgot yourself. It happens to all of us," Sir Edward pointed out.

"Your placement certainly occurred with a minimum of fuss," agreed Aunt Joan. "Mr. Gordon observed the entire procedure. He is completely satisfied. Take a proper look inside, Sophia."

She walked up to stand at the open door. Sir Edward sat facing backward against the far wall of the coach. His injured leg was propped up inside a roughly constructed, hinged wooden box.

"One of your aunt's grooms fashioned this contraption for me with Mr. Gordon's instructions," he told her with a grin. "It is called a fracture box."

"It appears your limb will stay immobile, encased in such a secure way," she observed. "Are you quite comfortable?"

"I am," he assured her. "Are you ready to leave? The trunks are stowed in your carriage with Hawkes."

"Yes, of course. Allow me to say my good-byes to my aunt and cousin." She turned away to confront them. "I enjoyed my visit, Aunt. Thank you so much."

"You're welcome, my dear." She gave Sophia a hug and a kiss on her cheek. "Tell your mother to write me. It has been several weeks since I received a letter from her."

"Of course," Sophia promised and turned to Charles. "Keep applying yourself to your studies, young man. You will want to join your brothers at Eton College as soon as possible."

"I promise to, cousin!" he answered. "It is my dearest wish to attend Eton."

"Oh, Charles, have you no thought for your poor mum?" Aunt Joan bent over to ruffle her son's hair. "What will I do with myself when you go away to school?"

"You can join Father in London!" Charles declared proudly.

Sophia smiled at her cousin's enthusiastic proclamation as she bent over to give him a hug. Certainly, her uncle would find no fault with such a scheme. "Good-bye!"

"Good-bye, Sophia, good-bye, Sir Edward," they both called out as she climbed up the steps into the carriage.

Sophia studied Sir Edward's outstretched limb stretched across the width of the carriage. "Where would you like me to sit?"

"If you wouldn't mind sitting over there next to the box?" He pointed and winced. "I rely upon you to warn me if it should become jostled during the journey."

"Very well." She wedged herself into the open spot next to the wooden contraption.

"Here, my lady." Josephine entered the carriage and handed her a shawl.

"Thank you." Sophia put the wrap down at her side. "Sit next to Sir Edward, please."

The carriage door shut firmly behind her maid. Moments later, the coachman called out his orders to his team of horses and the carriage rolled forward.

Sophia waved at her aunt and cousin one last time before reaching for her book and reclining back against the leather seat. She opened the cover, turning the pages until she found the spot where she had stopped reading the night before.

"I thought you planned to keep me company on the journey," Sir Edward grumbled.

Sophia closed the book and dropped it onto her lap. "I'm sorry. I intended to read for a while to give you an opportunity to rest."

He scowled. "My days have been continually filled with bouts of *resting* and loneliness. I wish to take advantage of your companionship and talk."

"Very well. What would you like to discuss?"

"I was hoping you could suggest a topic."

Sophia glanced outside at the passing scenery. She observed the flat, green fields lined with large elm trees and thought of something she was curious about. "You mentioned you wished to try new farming methods on your estate. Could you explain what you thought to do?"

He raised his brows. "I find your choice of words intriguing. Do you believe my endeavors to be fruitless?"

"You implied your mother refused to listen to your ideas or to continence them," she reminded him. "Did I misunderstand?"

He turned away to stare out of the window for a moment. When he faced her once again, his expression was bleak. "I regularly confront opposition from my mother whenever I suggest deviating from historical, practiced procedures on the estate. She believes the farming methods applied by my father and grandfather were successful, not requiring any adjustment."

She nodded her understanding. "Can you explain to me why you believe your intentions will be advantageous?"

"I will certainly attempt to make my case," he

assented. "Are you familiar with the ancient practice of leaving a field fallow?"

"Yes." She pondered what she knew of the subject. "I understand after continually using land for food production purposes, it was thought to be beneficial to leave a plot empty for a period to allow the soil to rest and recover."

"You are right as rain, but it is an antiquated practice." He sighed. "I wish to increase the number of cattle on my land. As more and more people move to London and other large cities in search of work, the demand for vegetables and beef will certainly increase. To support the additional livestock, I need to plant the traditionally fallow fields at Horsham House with turnips and clover."

"Those crops will provide enough food for the animals?"

"Not only will they supply forage for the cattle, but the turnips also discourage weed growth and the roots are excellent winter fodder when the store of reserves is typically low," he clarified. "Clover provides important nutrients for the soil, and it makes excellent pasture and hay fields. Keeping more animals also leads to additional supplies of milk and cheese as well as meat."

She frowned. "Taking care of and housing additional livestock, as well as overseeing the production of the food and the transportation of it to London is a daunting undertaking. Do you have a steward or other workers who are knowledgeable about the process?"

"It certainly is an involved process in the beginning." He grinned at her. "With that in mind, I observed my tenants as they worked in the fields as well as their interaction with the limited number of sheep and cattle on my land. I have discovered several men who would be qualified to assist me in the endeavor. My steward would help me by relaying my orders to the workers and advise me on the evolution of the project."

"I must admit, I am surprised. I had no notion of the thought and the extensive research you have put into accomplishing the venture. Surely, Lady Collins can recognize this as well? Have you explained the process to her?"

He grunted and stared down at his hands before looking up to gaze directly at her. "Mother has no interest in hearing my ideas. My father's solutions and objectives are all that matter."

"Even with my limited knowledge on farming, I can comprehend the need to change and adopt new practices as demand changes with population growth. I would insist Lady Collins listen to your ideas and reasons for change."

"That is easier said than done," he portended, glumly. "I am sorry. I should close my eyes and rest."

The remainder of the journey was accomplished with little conversation. Josephine had closed her eyes soon after they left South Hill Park. With her head propped back against the seat, she snored softly through her open mouth. Sir Edward slept restlessly from his spot in the corner. Sophia worried that her choice of topic for discussion had disheartened and agitated her traveling companion. After a stop at an inn, where the patient was efficiently removed and then returned to the carriage without mishap, and after partaking of some tea and cake, he roused himself enough to question her about the book she was reading. But even then, Sir Edward's attention wavered, and he seemed preoccupied by other matters. Their conversation tapered off and eventually ceased altogether. She attempted to read but soon realized she was not comprehending the words on the page in front of her. She leaned back against the seat and closed her eyes.

"We have arrived at last!" Sir Edward announced, as the carriage rolled to a stop in front of Horsham House. "Go inside and greet Mother, Lady Sophia. It will take some time for me to be unloaded."

"Very well." She picked up her book and reticule, slowly making her way to the open carriage door. Josephine followed behind her, carrying the pile of shawls. "I will enquire on the status of my coach as well. I note that it hasn't yet made an appearance."

"Hawkes will be upset." Sir Edward frowned. "Jensen told me they were right behind us at the last stop."

Sophia became aware of a pounding sensation from horses' hooves and the sound of a creaking vehicle. She stepped out of the carriage to spy her coach heading up the drive. "They have just arrived."

"Excellent! I will see you inside."

Sophia made her way up the steps to the front door, with Josephine following behind her. The portal opened wide as they reached the landing.

"Lady Sophia, welcome back to Horsham House," intoned the butler, Parley.

"Thank you, Parley. Sir Edward will arrive momentarily."

"Yes, I understand he requires additional assistance. I have instructed a groom to bring the push chair out to the carriage."

At that moment, there was a commotion at the bottom of the stairs. Sophia discerned Sir Edward was already sitting inside the wheeled contraption. Two grooms were positioned on either side of the chair and the valet held his master's leg steady, still incased in the fracture box. Hawkes walked slowly, facing backward, his feet groping for purchase on each step before he allowed the others to move forward. After many tense minutes, they reached the landing.

"Wonderful! Thank you, men, for your careful assistance," Sir Edward spoke out with obvious relief. "I am indebted, Hawkes. I don't know how I would manage without you!"

"Parley, have a footman assist Hawkes," Lady Collins commanded, suddenly appearing on the scene. "Edward, I have asked that the room off your study be converted into a bedchamber for now. I thought it would be much more convenient instead of having to carry you up and down the stairs."

"Very good, Mother. Thank you for your foresight. The arrangement will suit me admirably." He grimaced, turning to Sophia. "I will rest now and see you this evening."

She watched silently as Hawkes pushed the wheeled chair down the hallway and slowly turned the contraption to enter the study. The door closed behind them.

"I must ask you to join me in the drawing room for a few minutes, Lady Sophia. Here is my housekeeper to show your maid where to put your things." Lady Collins moved away from her, toward the stairs. "The servants are putting the bedchamber you are to occupy to rights. Camille has gone for a walk with Miss Cather. I received Edward's missive advising me of your intention to accompany him on the journey only an hour ago."

"I apologize for the short notice, my lady," she told her. "My determination to join Sir Edward was made at the last minute."

The other lady made no reply to her comment and Sophia followed her up the staircase.

The butler opened the door to the drawing room as they reached the top of the stairs.

"Thank you, Parley. That will be all for now." Lady Collins bustled inside and perched on the edge of a love seat near the fireplace. The door closed behind the butler. "Please sit down. I wish to inform you that I was confused by your decision to come here. While I hoped you would periodically visit my son while he remained at your aunt's residence, I never imagined you would accompany him on his journey home."

Sophia lowered herself into an over-stuffed chair nearby. "My aunt had the notion. She felt it was past time that I returned to London and thought to send me on my way in the company of Sir Edward. She felt I could keep up his spirits on the journey, as well as engage him in conversation to keep his mind off the injury."

"Indeed." Lady Collins pursed her lips and frowned at her. "I cannot imagine my son would be diverted by discourse related solely to yourself."

"Nor could I," Sophia acknowledged. "There was no mention of that. In fact, we discussed agriculture and livestock."

"You spoke of…?" Lady Collins' mouth dropped

open. She quickly shut it and cleared her throat. "You have shocked me, Lady Sophia."

"No doubt I will also overwhelm and outrage you with what I am about to say." She took a moment to determine the most credible way to get her point across. "I wish to ask something of you. Please inquire about your son's plans for improvements on the farm here. Allow him to implement his ideas. He needs to know you trust his judgement, knowledge, and research."

Lady Collins' brows rose alarmingly, and her nose wrinkled as if she smelled something rotten. "How dare you presume I need advice on how best to talk to my son!"

The notion that she should beg the lady's pardon crossed her mind at that moment. She thrust the thought aside. She must do this for Sir Edward. He would turn into an angry, purposeless, distrustful man if she didn't speak up for him. "Don't you see what you are doing, Lady Collins? You are crushing his spirit by refusing to hand over the management of the property on the estate to him."

"Crushing his...?" she repeated. "My son is in charge of the lands here."

"If he is in control, why do you refuse to allow him to experiment or attempt the new procedures?"

Lady Collins stiffened her spine and glared at her. "The estate and lands have always been profitable, guided by the time-honored traditions of my husband and his father before him."

"Do you believe they never experimented with their own ideas or attempted new methods? Life is not a stagnant thing, it is everchanging. To ignore that natural progression, we become frustrated and hopeless. Do not consign your son to such a horrible existence."

"When did you stop thinking of yourself and worry about the welfare of my son?" the other lady demanded.

Her question startled Sophia. She paused, going over the many conversations she and Sir Edward had shared over the past weeks. "My life changed when I was sixteen. I closed myself off from the world. I retreated into my own shell. When I came to realize I could not hide forever, I chose to pretend and deceive. Your son has shown me this was wrong. He has allowed me to love myself again, to be proud of who I am in truth."

The door swung open. Camille strode into the room. Miss Cather followed behind her. "Sophia! You are here! I couldn't believe it when Parley informed me. I had to come see you at once. Ellen is delighted as well!"

Lady Collins stood up, advancing to the open door. "I leave you ladies to your reunion. I will see you at dinner."

****

"Thank you, Hawkes." Edward reclined back against the pillows on the sofa in his study while his valet checked the position of his leg. The confining fracture box was stowed away, his foot now propped up on a stool.

A knock sounded on the door.

"Yes?"

"May I…I speak with you, Edward?" His mother's voice sounded strained.

"Of course," he replied. "You may go, Hawkes. Mother?"

She walked with a hesitant gait inside the room and

sat down next to him. "Edward, I don't know how to say...I didn't realize..."

"What has happened, Mother?"

She reached out to put a hand on his shoulder. "Will you tell me of your ideas for improvements on the farmlands here?"

"W...What?" The air rushed from his lungs. His gut lurched as if he had just been pummeled.

"I want to hear your plans."

He took a deep breath while studying her flushed countenance. "Mother, why are you asking this of me now? You have always refused to hear anything I had to say on the matter."

She sighed. "Lady Sophia has just berated me for not listening to your notions about improvements. She pointed out how damaging it would be to your well-being to be denied the ability to experiment and research. I realize I was wrong to insist nothing should ever change on the estate."

"I owe her my deepest gratitude." He blinked as beads of moisture formed in the corner of his eyes.

"Edward! Are you crying? She has done so much for you?"

"Yes, she has. Allow me to explain all she has accomplished, Mother."

Chapter Nineteen

After she arrived back in London, Sophia dutifully accompanied her mother to a few balls. Thankfully, many peers and their families had returned to their estates. Other than some obligatory dances with gentlemen who showed no interest in furthering their acquaintance, Sophia was left alone.

Even though almost two months had passed since she had left Sir Edward's estate, there had been few opportunities to begin her search for a house. She had studied two homes from the outside in Mayfair that had "to let" signs in their front windows. In one instance, after claiming an important errand, she managed to take her father's coach, with Josephine in attendance, to view a residence in a quiet neighborhood on the other side of Hyde Park. The house had proved costly and too large for her needs.

Presently, she sat in front of her writing desk intending to compose a note to Sir Raeford asking him to accompany her on another residence search. A knock sounded upon her chamber door.

"Come in."

Josephine strode inside the room. "Lord Breech is asking for you, my lady. He wants you to come to his study."

She sighed and placed the quill pen back in the stand. "Very well."

Sophia walked down the stairs to the hallway and opened the door to her father's study. She went inside. He stood at the drinks' table, pouring a glass of brandy. Her mother sat on the sofa. She handed a cup of tea to her without speaking.

"Sit down, Sophia," her father ordered, before taking a sip of his brandy. "I have excellent news. I have received a very gratifying offer for your hand."

"My...my hand?" she asked with confusion as she lowered herself into a chair. Her arm shook as she placed her cup on a side table.

"Yes, in marriage," he explained. "The proposal comes from a gentleman I have great respect for. You are very lucky to have received notice from him considering your advanced age."

"Who...who has offered to marry me?" she asked, perplexed. Regardless of her recent attendance at a few balls, after the many seasons she spent off-putting prospective gentlemen, no man in society would dare to contemplate making her his wife.

"I am very happy to tell you, I have agreed to Lord Rambolt's suit," he informed her in a cavalier manner.

"No! It cannot be true!" She put a hand to her mouth, gagging as she thought of his cabbage breath and musty-smelling clothes.

"I realize this event must be a great surprise to you. Several years have gone by since your come-out took place, and you never received an offer. Now that one has been procured, the thought of being mistress of your own home is overwhelming."

"No! No! Father, please do not say I must do this!" she begged.

"I have already assented to his proposal. As your

father, there can be no question of my right to do so," he roared at her, his face mottled in anger.

"It is a very favorable alliance, Sophia," her mother pointed out. "I must remind you, you will be turning twenty-one soon and cannot wish to waste away into a spinster."

"I will have no more coddling and indulgence!" her father bellowed. "You have had more than enough time to make your own choice, Sophia. I am through humoring your fits and starts. You are betrothed to Lord Rambolt. He is on his way here from his estate in Manchester. After a few stops at his other properties along the way, he plans to be in London in a little over a fortnight's time. Once a special license is obtained, you will be married on the following morning."

She stood up, knowing only one way to make her parents understand why she could not be anyone's wife. She must tell them her secret. "You do not understand. I cannot marry. When…when I turned sixteen, I thought I met a man I loved. We planned to marry. Something happened. I…I am no longer pure. I am not a maiden."

"Sophia!" her mother exclaimed.

"What? Who is this blackguard?" her father yelled. The remaining brandy sloshed in his glass as he dropped it on the table with a shaking hand.

"It is ancient history." She experienced a rush of confidence, acknowledging the unarguable validity of the circumstance. "What matters now is the fact that no man will accept a soiled bride."

"To the contrary," her father countered. He reached a quivering hand into the pocket of his waistcoat and brought out his handkerchief, mopping beads of moisture on his brow. "It is quite possible for a lady's hymen to break in other ways. Say nothing to Lord Rambolt. If he questions you after the deed is done, tell him you spent much of your youth on horseback."

She gasped. "You are incorrigible, sir!"

"I…I." Her father struggled to breathe, and his skin color had taken on a pasty white hue. Sophia took a step toward him. "Father, are you ill?"

Her mother rose from her seat, hurrying to his side to clutch the sleeve of his coat with a trembling hand. "Arthur, you must sit down!"

Without acknowledging her, he lurched to a nearby chair with faltering, stumbling steps to collapse onto the seat with a lethargic exhale. Several moments passed with only the sound of his labored, ponderous breathing filling the room.

"Please, Father, you must explain. I do not understand why you are so insistent that I marry with such haste," she pleaded.

"It…It." He struggled to continue.

"My dear! You are not well!" Her mother reached out and began to loosen his cravat.

"No!" he rasped as he batted her hand away. He slowly raised himself to a rigid, upright position against the back of the chair. His eyes opened wide, and he gazed directly at her before muttering, "It is past time I told Sophia what has happened. She must understand the reason it is imperative she marries as soon as possible."

"What has occurred?" She whispered the words, her throat felt tight and constricted.

"Several months ago, I made a foolish investment. At the time, I understood the funds would increase ten-fold in a matter of weeks. Instead, the money was used for nefarious purposes. It is gone, all gone. The mortgages on my properties are coming due. I must get the money to pay them. I cannot and must not lose the lands and estates that have been in our family for so many generations."

"I am very sorry to hear of this, Father. How does forcing me to marry Lord Rambolt solve the problem?"

"My father...your grandfather, left fifty thousand pounds in trust for you. The money is to be released to your care on your twenty-fifth birthday or on the day you are married, whichever comes first. As part of the betrothal agreement, Lord Rambolt will advance me twenty thousand pounds of the money."

"Grandfather left me...why did you not tell me of this?"

"He asked I not inform you of it. He wished the money to be a surprise, a comfort to you and not a constant expectation in the back of your mind."

She paced back and forth across the room. "I am unable to comprehend the plans you have for me, Father. You would consign me to a life of misery with Lord Rambolt without a qualm? Surely there is some other way to get the funds you require!"

"I repeat, a betrothal agreement has been made." He glared at her. "You will be married the day after Lord Rambolt arrives in London. Resign yourself to this, Sophia. There is nothing you can do to stop your marriage from happening."

Her heartbeat quickened, reverberating loudly in her ears. She squeezed her fingers tightly into her palms, her nails biting into the tender skin. There must be some way to avoid this terrible situation. Who could she ask for assistance? At that moment, she suddenly remembered Sir Edward's decree, "...*if you ever need my assistance, no matter how trifling, please write to me at Horsham House.*"

He was her only hope. She turned, sprinting to the door.

"Where are you going, Sophia?" her mother called after her.

"I...I must see...see to a...a personal matter," she choked out the words, slamming the door behind her.

****

Breaking her fast, four days after the messenger had ridden off with her urgent plea for help to Sir Edward, Sophia began to worry. She had received no response from him and was running out of time. Lord Rambolt would be arriving in London soon. She pushed her plate containing a bit of egg and half-eaten piece of toast away.

"Excuse me, Lady Sophia," the butler spoke from the threshold of the breakfast room. "Lord and Lady Breech wish to speak to you in the drawing room."

Her heart skipped a beat and she gasped for air. Surely Lord Rambolt had not arrived days before he was expected? "Th...Thank you. I...I will be with them momentarily."

She struggled to get up and out of her seat. She gradually came to her feet and steadied herself by clutching the back of the chair with a shaking hand. It was hard to believe her life would end this way. After all the years of living a pretense in order to avoid marriage and the resulting stigma of discovery, she found herself sold to a wealthy, aged peer who saw her as nothing more than a youthful woman capable of providing him with more children. And, if her father were to be believed, the fact she was no longer a virgin could be reasoned away with a simple, excessive horse-riding explanation.

She made her way out to the hallway and up the stairs to the drawing room. She gripped the knob, opened the door, and stepped across the threshold. Sophia kept her gaze on the carpet, afraid of who she might encounter inside.

"Sophia, we have been waiting for you." Her father's voice boomed from somewhere on the other side of the room. "Where have you been?"

"I…I was breaking my fast," she mumbled, clutching her stomach as a piece of dry toast that she hadn't adequately swallowed earlier suddenly lodged in her throat.

"Whatever is the matter, Sophia?" her mother inquired with impatience. "Come over here where we can see you."

She reached for her handkerchief, concealed in the side pocket on her gown, and coughed into it. The piece of bread broke free. She cleared her throat, tucking the handkerchief away. "I'm coming."

"I have something of great importance to tell you," her father announced, not waiting for her to make her way across the room.

"Yes, what is it?" Her question ended on a sigh as she lifted her gaze to study the perimeter of the space. No one else was present.

"I have received a message from Lord Rambolt. He expects to arrive in London in three days' time," he informed her. "He will obtain the special license and you will be married the following morning."

"Father, I beg you, please do not make me do this!"

A knock suddenly sounded, and the drawing room door swung open. The butler called out in a stentorian tone, "Sir Edward Collins!"

"I informed you we were not to be disturbed!" her father thundered, his complexion turning beet red.

"Edward?" Sophia swiveled around to face the open door, her mouth cleaving open in astonishment. He strode inside the room, walking forward with an elegant silver-topped cane at his side, his gaze only on her. She studied his familiar countenance. His luminous green eyes, thick, tousled dark hair. Her gaze drifted lower, and she found herself admiring his skintight buff breeches covering his hips, muscular thighs, and long legs. She started in surprise as she registered his tall form. It had been so long since she had seen him standing upright on his own two feet! His modish coat couldn't conceal the width of his shoulders or the powerful extension of his chest. Sudden erotic heat flowed over her as she acknowledged how truly handsome, magnificent he was.

"My dear." He strode across the room, without the use of the cane, before bowing in front of her with a gallant flourish. "I am sorry to be so tardy. The archbishop had a large audience of gentleman to confer with before he could see to our business."

"Business?" she murmured, still not quite believing in his presence.

"Why the special license, of course!" He winked at her and reached inside his coat, drawing forth the piece of parchment with a dramatic flourish. "We can be married immediately."

"How dare you! You presume to interrupt a private family discussion offering no word of apology or sense of remorse!" the Earl bellowed from his chair. "I order you to the leave the premises immediately."

Edward turned to face her father, unrolling the license so the seal of the Archbishop of Canterbury blazoned clearly for him to observe. "I must retaliate against your claim that I have no business here, my lord. I have a special license. As you can see, I will become your son-in-law before too many hours have passed."

"Sophia?" her mother gasped and reached for her fan, plying it up and down in front of her face in a shaky, sporadic motion.

"What kind of harebrained notion is this? My daughter is betrothed to another!"

"I am sorry to contradict you," Edward calmly replied. "Sophia agreed to our union several weeks ago."

"Impossible!" the Earl roared. "Sophia never once mentioned the occasion."

"Please explain, dear," her mother implored her, with a worried glance at her husband.

"I…I. We…"

"I have but lately recovered from breaking my leg in a riding accident," Edward broke in. "I couldn't give Sophia a firm date when I would be able to walk on my own again and travel to London. We agreed to keep our betrothal secret until the surgeon pronounced me fit and healthy once more."

"This is highly irregular, sir!" her father blustered. "I will repeat, I have already agreed to Sophia's betrothal to another suitor."

"And I argue that I have a prior claim to your daughter's hand in marriage as well as a special license in my possession." Edward turned to her. "My dear, go to your room and prepare for a journey. I will discuss settlement issues with Lord Breech."

Chapter Twenty

Sir Edward took her hand in his, helping her up the steps and into his carriage. He followed directly behind, settling beside her on the soft leather seat. Once the groom had secured the door, the coachman called out the horses and the vehicle rolled forward. Resting the cane against his leg, he turned to face her.

She gave him a glittering smile before letting a giggle escape from her mouth. "You were truly masterful! Did you see the expression on my father's face when you eloquently proclaimed you had already obtained a special license? I will never, ever forget it! I can hardly wait to describe the scene to Camille!"

"Camille is in Bath with my mother," he told her, softly.

"In Bath?" she frowned and gasped. "Oh, they have gone to visit Lady Collins' friend? I had intended to stay with Camille until I can arrange to let a house in London. My maid Josephine! We left in such a hurry. I must go back."

"Sophia." He paused to admire her flushed, rosy cheeks, her glowing violet eyes, trembling, full lips before reaching for her hand. "Josephine packed a bag for you. It is secured on the back of the carriage. We are getting married. I have an appointment with the vicar at Saint Pancras church in an hour."

"No!" She pulled away, glaring at him. "I cannot

marry! My reasons for not doing so are well known to you."

He took a deep breath. "I understand your stance about others offering advice on how to live your life, so I am not surprised you choose to argue with me instead of meekly accepting your fate. Please, Sophia, listen to me. What occurred when you were sixteen happened through no fault of your own. You lay with a man you believed would eventually be your husband. That is in the past. You must move on. In our case, I would point out there are other ways to be married besides the conventional method. We will remain friends. The only thing changing is we now reside under the same roof. I am eager for us to be each other's helpmates We can offer each other advice and suggestions when needed. I will see that you are provided a room near the kitchen in order to continue concocting your face cream. I intend to carry on implementing changes on the estate such as crop rotation, livestock additions, that I discussed with you previously, as well as other tenant and land improvements."

"I cannot do this!" She sobbed.

"It must be done," he insisted. "We will visit the bank after the ceremony. As part of your dowry, I agreed to turn over to your father the funds he needs to make payments on the mortgages, as well as other impending bills."

"It is not fair!" she exclaimed. "I looked forward to maintaining my own establishment in London. I'm certain you intended to meet and marry a woman of your dreams. A sweet lady to build a loving family with. We are both trapped for life in an exceedingly awkward situation."

"I had resolved to take my time to find a special woman to marry. I wished to be absolutely familiar with her likes and dislikes, her good qualities, as well as any irritating penchants," he admitted. "I never had the luxury of opportunity. I could only manage a fortnight or so during the season due to responsibilities at home. You are the only young woman, other than my sister, I am close to. After a rocky beginning and weeks of serious conversations and debates on a myriad of issues, I believe we are now staunch allies. Is this not a firm foundation upon which to establish and build a life together?"

"What you say makes sense," she acknowledged, turning away from him to face the window. She shivered, grasping at her shawl, pulling up it high across her shoulders. "But…"

He reached out to gently rub her shoulder with one gloved hand. "What is wrong, Sophia? Are you cold?"

"No…No." Her voice sounded hoarse, guttural. "I had an image…an image of Lord Rambolt…forcing me to…"

"Do not think of that," he admonished, as he put both hands at her waist in order to swivel her around.

She didn't resist. She turned to face him, wiping at a tear as it rolled down her cheek. "What…what about sleeping arrangements?"

"We will maintain separate quarters, of course," he answered, keeping his hands around her, while admonishing himself not to look at her full, trembling lips. The temptation to kiss her threatened his fragile composure. He cleared his throat. "I will eventually need an heir to secure the estate in the family. We can discuss that consideration once we have become more comfortable with one another."

"Very…well. Certainly, an heir is a requirement in your circumstance."

Her thin frame shuddered as she spoke the words. He loosened his hold at her waist to gently grasp her forearms. "Sophia, listen to me. We can contrive to make the best of the current situation and work together as a team. Or allow peevishness and discontent with our current course ruin any chance of knowing happiness together."

"Whoa!" the coachman called out the order and the carriage rolled to a stop.

"We have arrived at the church." Edward pulled his handkerchief out of his waistcoat pocket to dry the wet marks on Sophia's face left behind from her tears. "I asked Mr. Rudder to meet us here to serve as a witness to the ceremony. You recall him from the house party last year?"

"Yes, I remember." She slid down the seat away from him, reaching up to pat her hair and adjust the large comb holding the strands in place on the crown of her head. "Thank you for admonishing me. What you say is true. I promise to do all I can to make our union a successful one."

The groom opened the carriage door at that moment, letting the step down. Sophia gripped the leather hand strap at her side before standing up and making her way to the opening. She emerged outside with the groom's assistance, looking away from him toward the church.

He quickly climbed down, glancing up at the thick, gray clouds scudding nimbly across the sky.

"Sir Edward!"

He turned to see a tall, muscular gentleman dressed modishly in a bottle green frock coat, worn over a stripped celestial blue and white waistcoat, topped with an elegantly tied, crisp white linen cravat. His long limbs were covered in biscuit-hued nankeen breeches tucked into a shiny pair of Hessian boots. Edward bowed to him. "Mr. Rudder! Well met! Thank you for joining us on this important occasion."

The young man strode purposefully toward them and removed his top hat before executing a low bow. "It is a great honor to be a witness at such a happy event."

Edward reached for Sophia's hand, drawing her forward. "My dear, Mr. Rudder."

She curtsied to him. "Hello, Mr. Rudder."

He beamed at her. "You are looking breathtakingly lovely, as usual, Lady Sophia."

"Thank you for your kind words, sir."

"Shall we go inside?" Edward placed Sophia's hand on his arm, clutching his cane in his other hand before guiding her into the church, with Mr. Rudder following close behind.

They stepped into the cool, dimly lit interior. The scent of ancient, musty cloth and damp flagstone assailed Edward's nostrils. As they continued walking down the central nave, he noted the pile of glowing coals in the fireplace along the wall to the left. The white-washed walls contrasted with the dark brown wood on the rows of pews. At the foot of the nave, the vicar stood beside the podium, wearing a long, white robe.

"One moment." Edward released Sophia's hand and reached for the special license tucked away in his coat pocket. Grasping the rolled parchment, he drew out another tiny parcel wrapped in a handkerchief. He held the bundle out to Mr. Rudder. "The ring. You will be prompted to hand it over to me at the appropriate time."

He grasped the proffered item, wrapping his fingers around it. "I understand."

Edward turned back to Sophia, once again placing her hand on his arm. He glanced at her face, noting the rosy blush on her smooth cheeks. "Is something wrong?"

"No. You have thought of all the eventualities," she declared with a murmur in his ear.

"Sir Edward Collins, I presume?" the vicar addressed him in a booming voice.

"Yes." He guided Sophia forward. "Here is the license signed by the Archbishop of Canterbury."

The vicar adjusted his spectacles across his nose and reached for the piece of parchment. After studying it for a moment, he cleared his throat and looked directly at Sophia. "Everything seems to be in order. Am I addressing Lady Sophia Hampton, daughter of Lord and Lady Breech?"

She took a deep breath before replying. "Yes, that is correct."

"Are you of legal age to be married without the need of consent? Have you ever been married before?" The vicar quickly discharged his queries.

She gasped and gripped Edward's arm before responding. "Yes. No…No."

"Very well." The vicar considered her for a moment more before addressing him again. "I am Vicar Butterworth. I presume this gentleman is your witness?"

"Yes, he is. Mr. Rudder, sir."

The vicar grunted an acknowledgement and then pointed a boney finger. "My wife will serve as the other witness to the ceremony."

Edward turned to see a tiny woman wearing a bonnet sporting a white daisy dangling off the side, sitting in the front pew. She smiled at him while tapping the cover of a prayer book on the bench next to her with one hand.

"Everything appears to be in order," pronounced Vicar Butterworth, laying aside the license and picking up a large book with tattered pages from the podium. He cleared his throat. "Shall we begin?"

****

"Dearly beloved. We are gathered together here in the sight of God…"

Sophia squeezed her eyes shut as the words from the timeless service washed over her. She stood straight and tall, gripping Edward's arm as if it were a ballast. She feared she would collapse and fall to the ground if she released him. Her feet no longer had any sensation, the sounds of the vicar's booming voice reading the sermon were nothing more than a vague rhythm pounding in her ears.

"I will!"

She came to her senses when she heard Edward's firm reply. The vicar turned to her, his heavily lined forehead wrinkling with deep creases as he studied her over his spectacles.

"Wilt thou have this man to thy wedded husband, wilt thou obey him and serve him, love, honor, and keep him in sickness and in health so long as ye both shall live?"

She glanced up at Edward. He smiled at her and gently stroked her arm. She quickly looked away to stare at her feet. "I…I will."

More vows were spoken. She dutifully repeated the words when prompted.

The vicar placed her left hand on top of Edward's. "The ring, please."

Mr. Rudder stepped forward proffering the plain gold band nestled on the soft linen of Edward's handkerchief. "Here it is."

"Take the ring in your right hand, Sir Edward. Repeat after me. With this ring, I thee wed, with my body I thee worship, and with all my worldly goods I thee endow in the name of the Father and of the Son and of the Holy Ghost. Amen."

For some unknown reason, the exalting phrases repeated by Edward resonated in her head, flowing out from there to lodge like a glowing ember in a previously frozen section of her heart. She became aware the vicar had motioned for them to kneel. Her new husband gave his cane to Mr. Rudder before he gently clasped her hand and bent with her on the worn piece of carpet, placed over the hard stone floor in front of the dais.

"Those whom God hath joined together let no man put asunder. For as much as Edward and Sophia have consented together in holy wedlock and have given and pledged their troth either to other, I pronounce that they be man and wife together, in the name of the Father and of the Son and of the Holy Ghost. Amen."

Edward turned to her and kissed her cheek. They were married.

Chapter Twenty-One

They signed the church register duly witnessed by Mr. Rudder and the vicar's wife. Coins discreetly passed from Edward's hands into the vicar's outstretched palm while the others were busy offering their congratulations to his new wife. In short order, the three of them made their way back down the nave outside to the front porch of the church.

"Are you staying in London tonight?" asked Mr. Rudder.

"No, we are returning to Horsham," Edward replied. "We have some business to conduct at the bank first."

"You'd best be on your way." Mr. Rudder glanced up at the sky. "Hopefully, the rain will hold off until you arrive at your estate."

Edward studied the clouds above them, thicker and darker gray than when they had entered the church. "Unfortunately, we do not have time to celebrate the occasion with a glass of champagne. Thank you for serving as our witness to our wedding."

"You are very welcome!" Mr. Rudder bowed to them. "Lady Collins, congratulations! Sir Edward, I wish you both a happy future!"

He turned, striding away from them down the street.

Edward held out his arm to his new wife. "Shall we

take care of our business at the bank? Their offices are just around the corner. We should leave for Horsham as soon as possible. I don't like the appearance of those dark clouds presently swirling over our heads."

"I shall have to get used to my new name," she murmured before gripping his forearm, studying him with her violet eyes from underneath the brim of her hat. "You certainly should proceed with a good amount of caution whenever a severe rainstorm looms in your travels."

He chuckled. "Are you attempting to chastise me for my previous grievous error when I rode Seymour in the downpour a few months ago, madam?"

She smiled at him. "Not at all. But you, of all people are aware of the gravely, serious consequence of riding in that storm and suffering a broken limb."

"Very true, my dear." He opened the heavy door leading to the Bank of England's impressive marble-covered lobby and guided her inside.

Less than an hour later, Edward ushered Sophia across the threshold and outside onto the busy sidewalk.

"I never expected you to do such a thing for me!" she retorted.

Edward glanced across the street and located his coachman, Jensen, standing by the carriage. He lifted his arm, signaling him to bring the vehicle around. "Your grandfather intended that money to be yours, not used to reimburse your father for a foolish investment he made."

"All the more reason you should not be the one responsible for Father's imprudence!" she countered.

He stowed the cane under his arm and clasped her hand in his. "Sophia, I am your husband now. I have no intention of ordering you about or observing your every move. I promise to allow you space and freedom to live your life as you wish. But in this one instance, please allow me to have my way. It is important to me."

She sighed. "Very well. I did promise to make certain we have a successful marriage. I should not begin by starting an argument on our wedding day."

"Thank you, my dear. I appreciate your restraint." He grinned at her. "I know how much you enjoy trading barbs and witticisms with me."

She giggled. "Of course. I find myself required to put you in your place on occasion. It wouldn't do to have you turn into an arrogant windbag!"

"Undoubtedly a predicament I should avoid," he countered, taking her hand and helping her up the steps of the carriage.

Sophia made her way inside and settled herself, facing front. He followed, using his cane for extra support on the top step. He lowered himself, with a grunt, onto the seat opposite her. The groom shut and latched the door. Moments later, the sound of Jensen's voice could be heard calling to the horses and the carriage rolled forward.

"How is your injury? Does it pain you?"

He stowed his cane nearby and settled back against the leather squabs, taking a deep breath before replying, "I wouldn't describe the sensation as painful. Certainly, there is a stiffness when I have been standing for a lengthy amount of time. I am to use the cane to take pressure off my leg rather than as a tool to aid me. It wouldn't do to become too dependent on it when I am walking."

"I understand. You have certainly improved rapidly

in the short amount of time since I left Horsham House," she observed with a smile.

"I intend to cease using the cane entirely within the next fortnight," he vowed, as the carriage rolled forward, quickly gaining speed.

"I do not doubt your intention, but perhaps the surgeon will advise you to use caution," she pointed out. "It would never do to reverse the gains you have made by attempting to do too much too soon."

He studied Sophia for a moment before speaking. He greatly appreciated her practical, common-sense approach. "You are wise to counsel me in this matter. I have often chided myself for my heedlessness and for acting without due consideration."

She pursed her full lips and frowned. "Forgive me! I spoke out of turn. I never meant to instruct you on such personal matters."

He reached across the carriage to place his gloved hand on her knee. "Sophia, you are my wife. I appreciate your concern. Please, promise me you will never hide your opinions, thoughts and feelings from me."

Her lips curved into a wobbly smile. "Very well, I promise. I also pledge not to continually pester you. It would never do to have you regret your request."

"There is no chance of that happening," he reassured her as he removed his hand and sat back once more.

She turned toward the window. "It has become quite dark outside. The trees are but a dim, ghostly outline."

Edward pulled the drape back and studied their surroundings. "It appears we won't make it to Horsham

House before the rain begins."

Moments after his declaration, a crack of thunder reverberated followed by a streak of lightning across the blackened sky. The sound of a frightened horse's whinny resounded eerily inside the carriage.

Sophia shivered and gripped the leather strap affixed just below the window, as the coach swayed and bounced over a rough patch in the road.

"Are you cold?" Edward patted the empty spot next to him. "Come sit next to me. We can keep each other warm if we sit together."

"Very well." She stood up and crossed to the other side of the carriage, settling herself on the seat. Edward draped his arm across her shoulders, bracing her tightly against his side.

"There. Much better." He pulled back the curtain. "Here comes the rain."

"Perhaps it is only a passing storm?" she asked, hopefully. The drops first sounded with a light tapping against the roof of the carriage but quickly increased to a muted roar as the rain intensified. Sophia looked outside. Nothing was visible on the other side of the window except for a thick sheet of rain.

The carriage suddenly rolled to a stop and the communicating panel slid open above them. "Sir, there is a coach partially blocking the road up ahead. Looks like one horse was spooked and broke free of the traces. I can hardly see, and the mud is forming fast. Croydon is just ahead."

"We will stay overnight there and hope the storm is gone by morning. Stop at The King's Arms."

"Yes, sir!" Jensen shut the panel with a snap and the carriage slowly rolled forward.

Edward lowered his arm and reached for her hand. "I think stopping here is the best option, don't you? I will request separate rooms."

She squeezed his gloved fingers. "Yes. It is the best decision. I worry what might happen if we became stuck and had to walk to find shelter. You might reinjure yourself."

"Ah, but you would be at my side to attend to me." He chuckled. "I am thinking that would not be such an awful prospect."

She glared at him. "Please! Do not make a jest about it!"

He sighed. "You are right to chastise me. Lying on my back at the mercy of others was agonizing. I never wish to experience those sensations of utter worthlessness again!"

She scowled. "I understand. I hate to be fussed over on the rare occasions when I feel ill."

The carriage rolled to a stop. Edward released her hand. "Wait for me here. I will see to our rooms and then come escort you inside."

"Very well."

He stood up as the door opened. A servant swathed in a thick, wool scarf peered out from underneath his cap. Sheets of rain cascaded down upon his shoulders. "Step this way, sir. There be some large puddles forming already!"

Edward paused at the door, turning around to grin at her, a lock of his thick, dark hair drooping over one brow. "I promise I won't be long, but I cannot pledge to be dry when I return."

Sophia giggled. "I can't imagine anyone avoiding a dousing in this weather."

The door shut behind him and she sat back against the leather seat with a sigh. A stormy adventure to start her married life with Edward, only a few months after another rainstorm that was responsible for his injury and their haphazard reunion. Was fate at work here or was it simply coincidence?

The door suddenly opened once more. Edward stood outside, droplets of rainwater rolling off his broad shoulders. He stretched out one hand to her. "Come, my dear."

She came to her feet, reaching out to grip his gloved fingers. He guided her down the carriage steps and then suddenly, clasped her around the waist and lifted her over the muddied driveway, setting her down underneath a covered porch. "Edward! Be careful! You must not strain your leg!"

He chuckled. "No harm done, Sophia. Come inside. I have engaged a private parlor and ordered tea for us. The innkeeper promised to build up the fire so we may quickly warm ourselves and dry our clothing."

Edward opened the inn's door and steered her inside, down a dark, wood-paneled hallway. A short, stocky, balding man wearing spectacles waited for them by an opened door. "Good evening, my lady. Please come inside and warm yourself. My wife will bring your tea in a few moments."

The door shut behind him. Sophia walked over to stand in front of the hearth. She shivered as the welcome heat from the fire caressed her body. "This is lovely."

"I...I have something to tell you." Edward paused to clear his throat. "Apparently many other travelers sought shelter from the storm as well. There was only one room available here. I inquired about openings at the Green Dragon and the Crown Inn but nothing else was to be found. I can fashion a bed for myself on the floor."

"No!" She twisted around to face him. She could feel her cheeks flush, not only from the heat of the fire. "We can share a bed. I tend to sleep curled up in a ball on my side. There will certainly be plenty of room for us both."

"If you are certain." He studied her intently. "We could go on to Epsom."

"And take the chance of the carriage wheels becoming stuck in the mud or one of the horses injured? No, Edward. This arrangement is fine," she assured him, with a forced, confident manner.

"Very well. I will have our bags brought to the room. We will have our tea and then you may go up first and…" He stopped. "I'm sorry. Do you need me to send a maid to assist you?"

"No. I can manage." She looked away, to study the flowered pattern on the carpeted floor. "Perhaps you could request some warm water?"

"Yes, of course, my dear."

The door to the parlor opened and a short lady, wearing a clean white apron across her singularly large bosom and round, protruding stomach, entered the room carrying a tray. "Here you are, sir and my lady. I have given you some of my famous lemon tarts, just out of the oven they be! And cucumber sandwiches. Enjoy your tea!"

"Thank you." Edward held out a coin. "Will you see that our bags are taken to our room and some hot water be brought up as well?"

"Of course, sir. Thank you, sir!" The door shut behind her.

Sophia settled herself in front of the teapot and poured out the liquid. She handed Edward his cup. She studied the pile of sandwiches and plate of lemon tarts, doubting her ability to eat anything at present. Her hand shook as she lifted her cup to her lips. She had allowed herself to become soothed by Edward's assurance they would become comfortable with one another before taking the steps toward intimacy. Now they were forced to share a bed mere hours after their marriage.

"Will you have some, my dear?" Edward held up the platter of sandwiches.

"Yes, please." She reached out and chose a sandwich, placing it on her plate, as she chided herself for her apprehension. She trusted Edward. But then a sudden memory of his luscious kisses came to her. "Oh!"

Edward froze, a half-eaten sandwich suspended in the air in front of him. "Are you well?"

"Yes, yes." She lowered her teacup to the table. "I had a...a sudden twinge. It...It must be hunger."

He sighed. "I am very relieved to hear you say so. There is plenty here to settle your stomach."

"The tarts smell wonderfully delicious," she blathered, wondering how she would ever be able to swallow more than a few bites of the food. She managed to nibble on a sandwich, swallow half of one tart and took a sip of her tea. "Could you ring for someone to show me to our room? I am suddenly very tired."

"Of course, my dear." He gave her a warm smile. "It has been quite an eventful day. I intend to enjoy a glass of wine and will do my best not to disturb you when I join you later."

****

"Mmmm." The soft sheets on the bed cradled and caressed her backside. The blanket covered and supported her in a snug, warm cocoon. Not wishing to interrupt the blissful sensations, Sophia kept her eyes tightly closed. She reached out with one arm to nudge the pillow further down underneath the covers and…"Wh…what?"

"Good morning, Wife."

"Oh!" She jerked backward, thrusting one arm forward for balance. Her fingers brushed against velvety taut, muscular skin sprinkled with tufts of coarse hair. She quickly clasped her hands together and flipped over on the mattress to face the wall. "I am sorry!"

He chuckled into her exposed ear. "As you can tell, I'm not!"

The mattress dipped as he moved closer, draping his arm across her waist. She shuddered as waves of cold, and then hot sensations flowed throughout her body at his intimate touch. She wiggled away from him, and her bottom suddenly collided with a hard, jutting object. She froze.

"I warned you, Sophia."

She spun around to face him, groaning. "This isn't supposed to happen! For so many years, I told myself I had a broken heart and would never desire anyone ever again. I became a sham, a false person, knowing a lady who had lost her virtue could never hold the esteemed role as the wife of a gentleman."

"What did you say?" Edward sat up, the sheet

dropped from his muscular shoulders, pooling across his firm thighs.

She frowned at him, training her gaze on his face even as she knew a fervent temptation to look lower. "I pretended to be someone I wasn't. You knew of that."

"No, no! That is not what I'm referring to. You said you thought you *would never desire anyone again*." He scowled. "Is there someone else?"

She studied the rumpled blankets, unable to confront the chagrin and dismay she knew would be reflected in his eyes when she confessed. She whispered the words. "I regret I have to tell you this, but I promised to be my true self. I desire you, Edward."

"Look at me," he commanded in a firm, raspy tone.

She slowly moved to face him. A strand of his thick, curly black hair had fallen across his forehead, his deep, green eyes gleamed like freshly cut grass after a spring shower. "I…"

"Stop!" He crossed his arms over his chest and raised one dark brow. "Are you expressing *remorse* over the depth of your emotions for *me*?"

"Yes. I know…"

"Listen to me, my dear. I love you. I want to thank you for having faith in me. Because you believed in me, I was able to trust my instincts and decisions." He reached out to cradle her cheek in his hand before descending upon her, his warm mouth covering her quivering lips. She froze for the span of one frantic heartbeat in surprise before the erotic sensations took over her body. A tingling began in her toes and waves of awe-inspiring agitation followed, consuming her entire body. She raised herself off the pillow to compress her mouth against his. She couldn't get close enough to him.

Edward kissed her softly, investigating, sampling, baiting. His firm lips moved across hers in a gentle exploration. He kept his hand nestled against her face while slowly, tenderly, nipping and sucking her lips.

She moaned with pleasure, and he dropped his hand from her face to wrap it across her back. Acting without conscious thought, her own arms slithered up inside the open nightshirt, across his bare chest and around his neck. She pulled him down, her fingers tangling in his hair.

"Sophia." The soft murmur of her name sounded against her lips as he deepened the kiss, while coaxing her mouth open and gently caressing her tongue with his.

She moved one hand to his chin, rubbing the stubble there with the pad of her thumb while returning his erotic kiss. Then his movements slowed, and he released her, lying down next to her, propping himself up on the pillow with one elbow. He took a deep breath and grinned. "I take it you are no longer regretful you have feelings for me?"

She sighed, smiling up at him. "To the contrary, I am extremely happy and content. Thank you for urging me to drop all pretense and be myself. It is a joy to be your wife without the burden of enacting those falsehoods."

He chuckled. "Although you can certainly be entertaining when you adopt a role, you are exceedingly more attractive and desirable to me when you display your true character traits. It is hard to describe the intense joy I experienced when you said you desired me."

She blushed. "I love you, Edward! I was concerned I would scare you away if I mentioned that intense, all-consuming emotion."

"Scare me?" He gave her a lopsided grin. "Promise me you will never hesitate to say those words to me. I will never get tired of hearing you say, *I love you*."

"I promise. There is something else I am profoundly grateful for." She giggled as she reached for him under the covers. "I'm so glad we are married!"

He gasped, clutching her shoulders, slowly lowering her until her lips hovered just over his. "So am I, so am I!"

Author's Note:

Many of the things I wrote about in this story are true. George Canning bought South Hill Park in Bracknell, Berkshire in 1800. In 1809, the architect Sir John Soane was hired to make alterations to the principal floor of the house including the addition of a conservatory.

Joan Canning (Scott) was born in Scotland. She had two sisters, Henrietta and Lucy. I dropped Lucy from my story and created Lady Breech as Joan's other sister. The account of George and Joan's meeting at Walmer Castle is true as are the circumstances of their courtship. (I visited Walmer Castle in 2019 to obtain firsthand experience with the surroundings.)

They had four children, Charles being the youngest. The duel with Lord Castlereagh occurred in 1809 and George Canning received an injury in the thigh, as I described. However, his use of the push chair while recovering was my own invention.

A word about the author...

Cynthia Moore grew up in a small, southern California beach town. While many hours were spent lying on the sand, she always had a book in hand or a paperback tucked inside a bag ready to pull out and read after a quick splash in the waves.

Cynthia discovered British literature as a teenager. After reading most of the Victorian classics, she was introduced to English Regency period novels in 1987. It was love at first read. Since that time, Cynthia has read over four thousand fiction novels and owns a large collection of research books about the fascinating era.

She is extremely proud to have several published stories set during the Regency and resides in Southern California with her dog who is, not surprisingly, named Austen.

Lightning Source UK Ltd.
Milton Keynes UK
UKHW020828060223
416538UK00016B/1858